HAPPY

HOUR

By

Valerie Small

Copyright © 2017 Valerie Small

ISBN-13: 978-1547189359

ISBN-10: 1547189355

Published by:

Valerie Small

Edited by:

Dr. Ruth L. Baskerville

www.ruthbaskerville.com

Cover Design by:

www.ilovemycover.com

INTRODUCTION

This is the story of a very diverse group of single people living in a downtown condominium, where they meet in a central location most evenings at "Happy Hour." The concept of a "happy hour" has always been popular, particularly, though not exclusively among young people. Some of these residents become friends and some become lovers.

Some are bi-racial by birth, or involved as interracial couples, and some prefer lifestyles that don't involve heterosexual relationships. There's religion, indiscriminate sex, lies and clandestine betrayals, as these characters move in and out of each other's lives, like molecules attracting and repelling to stay in motion. Are you intrigued?

I describe in great detail each of the characters in this book, although the common thread among all of them is the condominium in which they live, and the interactions they have during and outside of "Happy Hour." My desire is to demonstrate through my story, which is loosely based on real characters, that in our modern society, "happy hour" is so much more than a place to get a drink and be casually social. It's also the meeting place, the life-blood of a small society within an upscale high-rise condominium.

It's real, it's raw, and it's relevant!

Valerie Small

TABLE OF CONTENTS

Chapter 1
Meet Armani Johnson, Esquire

It was the finest condominium complex in the downtown area, and though it had been open to residents for a decade, there was still a sizeable wait list of persons wanting to live there. Services included a sophisticated security system with a doorman present after hours. The living quarters ranged in size from one-bedrooms to three bedrooms, all with balconies. The lobby area was luxurious, with leather seating, long glass tables, oversize and tasteful art on the walls, and an abundance of live plants.

Residents can take advantage of laundry service, housekeeping service, and even dog-walking service. Oh, yes, this was a pet-friendly condominium, which was a major reason for the wait list of people trying to become residents. There's no solicitation allowed, which is the second reason people want to live here.

The current residents have shared this building for at least two of the ten years since it was built. Everyone knows at least the first names of everyone else, and some have formed deeper relationships. Even those who don't drink frequent the popular "Happy Hour," which is held monthly in a spacious lounge to the left of the lobby. It's stocked with a full service bar, and the two bar tenders also provide light refreshments that are salty enough to keep customers drinking longer than they intended when they came to "Happy Hour."

The other natural gathering place for residents is in the mailroom. Everyone checks mail daily, so folks are bound to run into each other as they come and go in the mailroom. It has become a "mini-Happy Hour," only without the alcohol!

So who are the people lucky enough to live here? Let's begin with Armani Johnson, Esquire, who is a divorce attorney who looked like actress Meagan Good, only taller. Armani was a "no-nonsense" woman who nearly always got her clients what they asked for. She was sexy and unafraid to use her femininity to her advantage when dealing with judges, prosecuting and defense attorneys. She purposely wore short skirts and shirts that buttoned down the front and showed cleavage, and high heels that accentuated her long, toned legs.

She was very smart, mind you. However, she was very much a woman with physical appeal, and she knew how to use it to her advantage before she met her husband, Truitt Johnson, Esquire, who put her through a terrible divorce a few years ago. He left her for another woman, and that broke her heart. The way she was able to cope with her grief was to become fully engrossed in her law practice. Armani Johnson gained the reputation of being a "revenge attorney" who would definitely be the one to choose if a scorned woman were looking to take everything except the shirt off her soon-to-be-ex-husband's back!

Armani enjoyed listening to music in general, but had a few artists she especially loved. She hardly ever watched television so on the many occasions where she brought her work home, she usually had music playing in the background with the television on, but muted. When she did watch television, it was reruns of *Flip Wilson, Richard Pryor, Carol Burnett, Martin* or any of those old, naturally funny comedies that don't seem to be replicated in the current television lineup. When she chose to watch the news, it was one of the local networks or *CNN*.

Nearly every day, Armani hit the gym for a workout. She would play Nina Simone's, *"I Put a Spell on You"* while she put on her work out clothes, and then as she prepared to leave home, she would listen to Tina Marie's, *"Oooh La La,"* Alicia Keyes' *"Fallen,"* and LL Cool J's, *"Doin' It."* One particular morning, just as she was about to leave for that workout, Prince's, *"Do Me Baby"* was coming on the stereo she was about to turn off. Well, she couldn't walk out on that song because it always reminded her of the times her ex-husband went down on her until she had an orgasm. Armani aroused herself by gyrating to the music and then masturbating. She washed her hands and left to get a good work out at the gym.

Armani was secretly dating a married federal prosecutor. Both of them were high-profile people, so discretion was of the utmost importance. She had a policy of not dating anyone in her profession or business, but she just couldn't resist this guy's charm. So far, they had been dating for three months without being seen out in public, because they realized that both their reputations were on the line.

Just as Armani and her married prosecutor companion thought they had escaped notice from those in their immediate circles, one of the judges who mentored Armani while she was in law school noticed how she was looking at the prosecutor while at a meeting. The judge told her he'd like to meet with her when they were done.

He warned her that if they were in a relationship, it could be very damaging to her career. He added that she needed to be careful because she was well respected in the court system, and this could jeopardize her career.

Armani tried to play it off, as if the judge who knew her well had misjudged her. But she realized immediately that her efforts were futile, so she politely smiled and allowed the judge to finish his gentle chastisement of his former mentee. He cared about her and didn't want her to lose everything she worked so hard for. He ended the conversation by saying he didn't mean to pry into her business.

Armani knew she was "caught," but much like a child who continues to feign innocence for a crime just committed, she simply thanked him for his concern and walked out his office to go home. While driving home, though, Armani was thinking the judge was right, and maybe she should end this affair. Affairs with married men never end well for the mistress, and, truth be told, Armani Johnson was the "other woman" for whom men don't leave their wives, despite countless bedroom promises to the contrary.

Armani was basically a private person, so very few persons knew that her ex-husband left her for another woman while she was in law school and working long hours simultaneously. Armani admitted to herself that back then, she didn't give much time to her marriage because she was thinking ahead to their future.

Her husband, Truitt, was a criminal defense attorney who also devoted little time and attention to nurturing their marriage. He did what most men did – took the easy way out by coming home every night, while cheating on his wife. Like so many lying, cheating men, Armani's husband didn't know how, or didn't care to be discreet. So the couple pretended the marriage was fine, until everything ended in divorce.

Still, she couldn't believe it when he told her he was divorcing her for an acquaintance whom they both knew. After all, both of them had worked hard at pretending to be a happily married couple, and the arrangement of seeming happy in public, but sleeping in separate quarters at home was working just fine. Why did he have to mess things up by actually requesting a divorce?

So Armani Johnson was out for revenge after her marriage ended. She was going to do to someone what was done to her, knowing damn well it wasn't right. It was probably a kind of "conflict of interest," too, since her duty was to focus on the facts when in a courtroom. Emotionalism was not a quality expressed by a seasoned attorney of her caliber. She promised herself silently that she would work on her temperament and bias, as she represented devastated wives suing cheating husbands for divorce.

By the time Armani arrived at her condominium, after a morning workout, a day of pressure as an attorney, and an unwelcome conversation with the judge who mentored her in law school, she knew without a doubt that this affair with the prosecutor wasn't going anywhere. However, she didn't care that he was married because her plan was to let him think he was special, then drop him like a bad habit. No doubt, Armani thought that would make her feel less hurt about her own failed marriage. It wouldn't.

When this prosecutor first started flirting with her, she played hard to get. Within a short time, she started conversing with him on different cases in which he was involved, and found him interesting and attractive. They had a few drinks at dinner one night, and her flirting turned to genuine passion. She started looking at him differently. He said all the right things by telling her he was in a bad marriage, but couldn't leave his wife because he had an image to uphold.

Armani took a walk to clear her head, and before returning to her apartment, she stopped by the florist a block away to pick up some fresh flowers that she loved to put in a vase on her cocktail table. A quick trip to the nearby grocery store to pick up some Italian bread to go with the spaghetti and meatballs she was making for dinner, and she was finally ready to head home.

Once inside the building, she remembered to check her mailbox. While getting her mail, she saw the notice about "Happy Hour" that evening, and she knew she would be going. It was her once monthly time to enjoy the companionship of fellow residents within their luxury condominium.

Actually, it was quite amazing that when she entered the building, all Armani wanted to do was get inside her unit, kick back and relax over dinner. However, there was something about the words *"Happy Hour"* that always gave her new energy. She thought she might invite Keo, who was a friend she met at the gym a year earlier. Maybe she would just go alone and see who showed up. We'll see!

Chapter 2
Gucci Mancini and Miss Dior Blue

Gucci Mancini was a former actor, female impersonator, and drag queen who knew he was gay at an early age. He didn't have to "come out" to his family, since his mother and father sensed he was different when he was very young, but loved him just the same.

His parents enrolled him in drama classes, thinking it would help him be the best he could be if he could act out his fantasies before live audiences. Gucci loved acting and was so talented that he went on one audition after another until he landed a role in the Broadway production of *The Wizard of Oz,* playing the cowardly lion.

Gucci was so credible as an actor that audiences loved him and cheered for him loudest when he took his bow during curtain call. He went on to get larger parts in musicals such as *Hairspray* and *Wicked*. Gucci became famous almost overnight, not only for his acting skills, but also for his sense of style and extravagant costumes. He appeared in a few sitcoms and was nominated for a coveted *Tony Award.*

People just loved Gucci, being drawn to his personality as much as his talent. He was grateful to his fans for their support, and always posed for pictures with them and signed autographs when asked. He was slightly overweight, had those eyes that always looked like they made his face smile, and he had the slightest hint of breasts under his fitted shirts. He was pretty tall, with a naturally soft voice that made you feel safe and happy around him.

He loved acting but was most passionate about doing impersonations of different women and Cher was his favorite. He also loved performing as a drag queen and participated in the *DIVA Awards* and won *Bell of the Ball* his first year. He was inspired by RuPaul's and Lady Bunny's careers because they were the best at what they did in drag.

Gucci was always teaching someone about acting and mentoring some of the "newbies" on how to do makeup, sew, and strut across any stage with poise and confidence.

Gucci lived in the condo at 1400 South for six years, and was considered among the first tenants in this classy, upscale residence. He knew the names of almost all the residents, making it a point to be the self-appointed "welcome committee" as new tenants moved in.

He was a kind and gentle soul who was involved in many causes. When he wasn't working, he volunteered at a soup kitchen feeding the homeless. He made a lot of his clothes and even designed clothes for his gay friends in New York. Most of them had grown up feeling like misfits and some had a sad story to share. Gucci was the exception, since his family accepted him for who he was and attended most of his performances. Gucci could do make-up better than any woman. He was passionate about theatre, music and art, so he was a big supporter of the arts through contributions and patronage.

Gucci met his neighbor, Miss Dior Blue when he was stepping on the elevator after getting his mail and she was getting hers. He was looking down while sorting through each envelope in his hand, when he literally bumped into Miss Dior. All his mail fell to the floor, and she helped him pick everything up. He apologized and told her he was embarrassed and to please forgive him. Dior jokingly said, *"Next time pay attention to where you're going,"* and they both laughed.

Gucci introduced himself as the "Chairman of the Welcoming Committee-of-One" at 1400 South. Dior laughed again. Miss Dior Blue was a boy child born to Taiwanese parents who didn't understand why he wanted to look like a girl, and why he hated taking pictures as a young boy. They had him in the Boy Scouts, which was a good thing because he learned survival skills and self-discipline. Then they enrolled him in karate, where he earned his way to a black belt. Dior Blue was a "bad ass," but one would never know since he was so soft-spoken and feminine.

Dior was miserable as a young boy because he loved make-up and dressing dolls with clothes he designed and sewed. Naturally, his parents and seemingly his whole society frowned on everything he held dear.

When he turned sixteen years old, he ran away, hitchhiking half way around the world and ending up in Philadelphia, where he was living in homeless shelters and on the streets. He had no plans to contact any members of his family again, so he felt safe as a transgender.

Dior presented himself to everyone in Philadelphia as "Miss Dior Blue," and *she* started working at a department store as a stockroom clerk. She loved it. She liked getting up and going to work, earning her own money and being respected as a hard-working young woman. For the first time in a long time she was happy. She was making minimum wage, but handled her money efficiently in hopes of leaving the shelter and getting her own apartment.

One day while she was working, her supervisor came and asked her if she could talk to her. Dior thought her sexual identity had been compromised, so she was a nervous wreck. The supervisor asked if she ever thought about modeling, to which Dior responded with a sigh of relief that she had thought about it but didn't know how to go about it.

The supervisor told her that someone from the community relations/special events department would be in touch with her about modeling in a trunk show. Dior wasn't familiar with a "trunk show," but was so excited and felt like she had the looks to be a model and could possibly pull this off.

A woman by the name of Ms. Mita came to see her and was staring at Dior in a way that made her feel as if she wasn't going to become a model. Ms. Mita was actually sizing her up. *"Honey, you'd be perfect for the show, and with a name like 'Dior' and the looks of a Tawainese model named Lin Chi-Ling, you'll show up all the other models. You're hired!"*

This was the start of a fabulous modeling career. Dior became a top model and was immediately in demand because of her unusual beauty and exotic look. Before she knew it, she was traveling the world at just nineteen years old. When occasionally asked about her family, she would simply say they still lived in Taiwan.

When she got her first big six-figure check, she sent money to some friends who had taken her in, and the shelter where she stayed when she first arrived in Philadelphia. Since she had no established credit, the uncle of her new friends co-signed for her to move into the condo downtown. That's how she became a resident of 1400 South.

Gucci and Dior stood in the lobby getting to know each other. She told him he looked familiar, and he told her he used to live in New York and was a stage actor. Dior volunteered that she used to model, and Gucci interrupted her. *"Used to! I just saw you on the cover of Vogue!"* Dior smiled and put her pointer finger to her lips and said, *"Shush, no one else has recognized me here yet."*

When not in drag, Gucci Mancini looked like Tim Gunn, from the *Project Runway* show. He was very distinguished and handsome. Dior complimented him on his fashion sense of casual slacks with a *Polo* shirt and loafers with no socks. Gucci responded, *"I look even better as a female!"*

They didn't realize they had been standing at the elevator almost fifteen minutes. Gucci told Dior to call or stop by, and he'd make her a good meal she'd never forget because he was an excellent cook.

Gucci saw the notice in the elevator about Happy Hour that evening, and he decided he would invite his good friend, Katherine Clyburn. He knew her when she was "Labelle Beaumont," and now she was married to the rising star attorney Dale Clyburn, whom Gucci didn't care for. There was something ugly about his spirit, Gucci thought when he first met Dale. On the other hand, he adored Katherine.

He knew it was last minute but when he called Katherine, she gladly accepted saying she was free since her husband, Dale said he was going to watch a hockey game with his pastor. They decided to meet in the lobby of 1400 South and walk into the Happy Hour lounge together.

Gucci and Katherine had attended a few events she organized at the Art Museum at which she served on the Board of Directors. He was glad she would be joining him because it was public knowledge that Katherine and Dale Clyburn were having marital problems. It was public knowledge to those who knew the couple, but outsiders continued to admire them as the "alpha couple."

Gucci agreed to meet Katherine in the lobby at 6:00 p.m., but he had a few errands to take care of first. When he got on the elevator to leave the building, Miss Dior Blue was in the elevator too. She lived on the floor above him.

Dior noticed the sign about Happy Hour and asked Gucci if he was attending. He told her he was going, and bringing a friend. She told him she was going also, and she was glad she'd have him to talk to, since she had yet to meet most of the residents in the building. Gucci promised to introduce her to everyone he knew, adding that he knew plenty of people there!

Everyone thought Gucci had it all, and at one point he did have a successful career and a lot of material things. But one thing he didn't have was love, and he often felt lonely at the end of a day. He hoped to meet someone at Happy Hour with whom he could form a mutual bond of love. Maybe that was asking too much of life, but Gucci was an optimist, so he believed love was possible. He knew a lot of people and had many friends and acquaintances, but he wanted a companion--someone to love, travel and grow old with.

Gucci finished his errands and returned home to dress for Happy Hour. He couldn't decide if he was going to dress as a man, a woman or drag queen, but then he decided to go as himself. Once dressed, he was feeling good, and ready to mix and mingle, so he started out the door, heading for the lobby to meet Katherine Clyburn. He was also looking forward to seeing Dior Blue at Happy Hour. There was something confident, yet fragile about her that made Gucci feel like he should protect her as a big brother would.

Gucci arrived in the lobby at just about 6:00 p.m., and just as he was walking toward the door, Katherine entered and he escorted her into Happy Hour. He didn't see Dior right away, but he hugged Armani Johnson. Those in attendance went wild with excitement to see Gucci, who was touched and honored by the reception the tenants gave him. Gucci Mancini was the most famous celebrity living at 1400 South.

Dior went over and gave him a big hug as if they were old friends, and he introduced Katherine to her. Dior told Katherine how beautiful she looked, and Katherine complimented Dior on her natural beauty, telling her she had seen the face of Dior Blue on the cover of the latest *Vogue* issue.

Gucci accepted all the applause that came his way, and when they finally stopped, he was free to work the room. He recognized members from the *Philadelphia Orchestra* and the *Philadelphia Ballet* Company. The building was full of important people who may not have mingled with each other much, but who seemed to gravitate towards Gucci. Gucci asked Katherine and Dior if they wanted a drink, and they all walked to the bar.

Some residents recognized Katherine Clyburn too, because of her generous support of the arts and her service on the board at the Art Museum. They walked to the bar and each ordered a glass of wine, with Dior telling Gucci and Katherine she was so glad she came.

While Katherine and Dior were in the ladies' room, Gucci saw a handsome guy talking with two of the residents. He knew one of them was Mercedes Johannson, and he knew she was a flight attendant.

When Katherine and Dior came out of the restroom, Gucci noticed the way the guy was staring at Dior so he decided to introduce everyone to him. The handsome guy was Keo Staffort, who seemed to be getting a drink for his date, Mercedes, because she suddenly appeared to pull him back to the table at which they were sitting alone.

All the residents and their guests enjoyed the monthly Happy Hour because it was a time to unwind, get to know neighbors and their friends better, and exchange numbers for networking purposes. Gucci would have liked to get Keo Staffort's number, but Keo was decidedly straight and wanted only the company of women.

The morning after Happy Hour, Miss Dior got a call from her agent, asking her to model underwear for a lingerie company. She knew that one day, she would take the really bold step of having the surgery to make her a complete woman, but those were long-range plans and her career was moving faster than she could ever have imagined. This was a real dilemma because her physical appearance in underwear was that of a man.

She told her agent she'd get back to her because she wasn't feeling well and needed time to think about it. Her agent told her this was a big deal, and if she didn't do it, she would regret it. The shoot was to take place in a few days, so her agent told her to get some rest and call back as soon as she could.

Dior needed someone to talk to, and thought of Gucci Mancini first. She called him and asked if they could meet for coffee right away. Gucci sensed something was wrong, and he stopped what he was doing to meet Dior.

She told Gucci her situation, and he said he knew she was a transgender when they met at the elevator. *"We who are comfortable in our skin as male and female can spot the folks living 'non-traditional' lifestyles. I never judge, lest….well you know the rest of that quote."*

Dior confessed, almost through tears, that she wanted many times to tell her agent she was transgendered, but she couldn't bring herself to say the words. She was adored by all her photographers and growing number of fans, and she was making more money in a month than her parents made in a year. She didn't want to ruin any of this.

She never considered the possibility of doing a lingerie shoot, but Ms. Mita said she would regret it if she didn't accept the job. Maybe she should consider giving up modeling, then have her surgery and live her life as a complete woman. Oh, but she didn't have the kind of money she needed for that operation, which is why she didn't want to end her modeling career. What should she do? She finally stopped rambling and sipped her coffee to allow her new, confidential friend to speak.

Gucci suggested she tell them the truth when she was confident enough, but she didn't seem ready to do so that day. He admitted that only Miss Dior knew what she was going through, but he hoped Ms. Mita would understand if she loved Dior like family. Also, Dior was making a lot of money for Ms. Mita and everyone else connected to her modeling shoots.

On the other hand, Gucci had to admit that he had friends whose family didn't want any parts of them being gay, and the drag queen thing really turned some of them off. Being different from what society considers normal and correct is tough. Gucci told Dior that until she decided to do otherwise, she was a beautiful woman who could "tuck her stuff" and do the lingerie shoot. But regardless of how things turned out, she would always be his little sister and he would protect her.

Dior gave him a big hug and thanked him for being such a great friend, and laughed a little when she awkwardly said she would "tuck the junk" and deal with the uncomfortable feeling long enough to do the lingerie shoot. She would tell Ms. Mita that, though she seemed uninhibited strutting across the stage under bright lights, she was really a private person who preferred not to do lingerie shoots in the future.

Chapter 3
Dale and Katherine Clyburn

Katherine Labelle Beaumont met Dale Clyburn at a dinner party thrown by the Governor and his wife. Katherine's last name was quite famous, since her father was a Count in England, known for philanthropic adventures all over Europe. He was regularly lauded in the press, and Katherine was well aware that when she gave her full name, eyebrows raised and heads turned in her direction.

Dale was immediately attracted to Katherine, thinking she was a Jackie Kennedy "look-alike" -- gorgeous, classy and someone anyone would want to bed and wed. Of course he knew of her wealth and social status, but that's not what attracted him to her. He fell in love "at first sight," as they say. They were both single, and Dale had just won a high profile case, so the night of celebration was all about him.

Dale mingled among the guests, making sure to conduct small conversations with all those who attended. He was ambitious, and part of his mingling was that he was always thinking about future contacts and what people could do for him. But he was also flattered that such a distinguished group of persons turned out for a party in his honor.

Dale was heading back to where Katherine was sitting when he spotted Pastor Elvis Paisley, who was the pastor at Dale's church. Dale was annoyed, since he wasn't aware his pastor would be in attendance. The pastor never called to respond to the invitation, though it clearly asked for an RSVP. Pastor Paisley looked out of place for a number of reasons, the first of which was that he was wearing his collar. People were laughing and drinking alcohol, and it seemed a little odd to more people than Dale Clyburn that a man of the cloth would be at this kind of gathering.

Dale took a deep breath, swallowed the contents of the drink in his hand, and moved towards his pastor. Dale firmly took his pastor's arm and ushered him to a corner of the room where there were no people. Dale whispered, *"What are YOU doing here?"* Pastor Paisley smiled and said he was there to salute the famous attorney Dale Clyburn, like everyone else in attendance. He also reminded Dale, with a slight smile, that Dale belonged to Pastor Paisley's congregation.

As Dale turned to leave Pastor, he heard, *"Besides, I've got 14,000 reasons to be here!"* Dale spun around and began to raise his hands as if to actually hit his pastor. He quickly composed himself, saying under his breath, *"I don't know what you're talking about, but you're no longer welcome at my celebration. Time for you to leave!"*

Dale moved away from him in disgust, just as one of the guests caught Dale's eye and followed it to Pastor Paisley. The guest looked confused, but surmised that something was wrong between the two men. Then the guest took another drink from the tray the waiter was carrying, and went back to being happy. Shortly after that, the pastor left.

Katherine had come to the dinner party with one of the male board members from the Art Museum, since her husband, Dale was coming straight from court. She assumed the wifely position by his side, making small talk with everyone who stopped to congratulate Dale on winning a difficult case.

Katherine was bored, but wore a convincing plastic smile that told everyone that all was right with the world! Her mind went back to a celebration similar to this one, where Dale Clyburn pursued Katherine Lebelle Beaumont. She didn't protest. In fact, she liked the attention, and before she knew it, they were engaged in a conversation both of them enjoyed.

Dale flirted with Katherine that whole night, then asked her out the next evening. She accepted, and "the rest is history." They had a short courtship before marrying. They were among the happiest couples in lawyer circles, considering the fact that half of the men were divorced, with more than half of those owing their empty wallets to Divorce Attorney Armani Johnson.

Katherine wondered when the passion left her marriage, and why her husband felt the need to creep at night, when she was willing to supply all his needs. She realized she was missing too many bits of conversations, and before she said something inappropriate or stupid, she stopped reflecting on her past and joined the present conversations in honor of her rising star husband, Dale Clyburn.

Armani Johnson also attended the party for Dale Clyburn. Members of the State Bar Association supported each other, as one or another got promoted. Armani knew several of the attendees at Dale's celebration, since she had made a name for herself taking on high profile divorce cases where she sued some of the lawyers in the room after their wives had contacted her in distress. Those men were careful to mingle outside of Armani's social space, since they had paid high prices to get out of their marriages.

Nevertheless, the protocol was that everyone was cordial, civil and respectful at events like this one. Also, Armani Johnson would never think of violating the confidentiality clauses attached to those many divorce settlements. She had to admit to herself that there was a sadistic pleasure in mingling with the men she had pummeled in court. She liked the power she wielded.

Dale and Katherine Clyburn were well known throughout Philadelphia as a "power couple." Each was established before their marriage, and after they married, they had collective access to a pretty large group of important individuals. Dale was a "hotshot" prosecutor with an impressive record of winning all his cases to date, and despite his success, he maintained a pleasant demeanor among colleagues for the prosecution and the defense. The Mayor of Philadelphia and several judges were often seen at lunch or dinner with him, and he brought his wife as often as he dined alone with the Honorable Mayor.

Katherine Clyburn was known as a lovely hostess who planned elaborate dinner parties at their home. It was considered special and important to be invited to one of the Clyburn dinner parties. Everyone in the legal and arts communities enjoyed the company of Dale and Katherine. Most couples considered them to be the "alpha couple," as close to perfect as two people becoming one could get.

Despite appearances, within two years, Dale and Katherine's near-perfect marriage was in trouble. Dale had a reputation with the ladies before he met Katherine, and he probably intended to give all that up for the love of his life. However, his testosterone overpowered his reason, and, while he loved his wife dearly, he reverted to his habits of creeping late at night into and out of some woman's bed.

At first, Katherine accepted Dale's lies about working through the night on a particularly difficult case. Sometimes, he pretended to be out of town for a couple of days, giving him real freedom to cheat without being seen in public. But he was simply away from her home and her bed too often, and so she rationalized that she loved him no matter what, and this was the way her life would be.

Katherine kept herself busy by continuing to serve on the Board of the Art Museum, and to plan and host elaborate dinner parties for Dale and his colleagues. They were part of an elite social circle, where there was always a "black tie gala" or social affair requiring their presence as a power couple always invited to the party.

Katherine had tried hard for two years to just be Dale's happy wife, and she refused to complain out loud about anything because she enjoyed their lifestyle. She also traveled abroad, looking at various exhibits that might be brought to the Art Museum for a season. The travel kept her busy, but also made her feel uniquely important because she alone made decisions on what would be featured at the Art Museum.

When Katherine Clyburn had had enough, she reluctantly decided to retain a good attorney to advise her whether or not she had a strong enough case to sue Dale for a divorce. She was ambivalent about actually getting a divorce, and needed to confide in a caring female divorce attorney to help her decide her options.

reaching for a tissue to wipe her forehead. She thought, "Why did I say, 'I'm sure I can help you.' I can't help HER!"

Chapter 4

Armani Johnson and Dale Clyburn?

Armani met Dale before he was appointed as a State Prosecutor. He used to work on bankruptcy cases. She had a few clients who spent all the money Armani worked so hard to get for them from their divorce settlements. They had to file for bankruptcy, and ended up being referred almost exclusively to Dale Clyburn. Dale attended a certain charity event without his wife, Katherine, and when he saw Armani, he took advantage of being "single" and approached her with a mind to flirt.

Dale had been secretly attracted to Armani for a while, but never approached her because, first, he was married, but second, she presented a rather gruff and standoffish demeanor to some men. Dale's ego couldn't stand being bruised, if he should approach

Armani and then be rejected by her. So he proceeded with caution.

Armani was sitting in a corner next to someone who had just gotten up when Dale looked in her direction, so she was alone at that moment. Dale walked over to her and complimented her on her outfit, which was a business suit with a split up the skirt. Her blouse, however, was a glittered print that made everyone close to her stare at her chest before looking away with embarrassment. Her heels accented her long legs, and when she crossed one leg over the other, the slit in her skirt showed almost all of one thigh.

There wasn't a physical attraction on Armani's part at first, but she did find him to be charming and a gentleman. They engaged in a technical conversation about a high-profile case that was recently publicized, asking one another how they would have handled it. After a few drinks, Dale asked Armani for her phone number and she gave it to him. Both of them knew Dale was "happily" married, but neither one cared. It was understood that when Armani surrendered her phone number, she would at some point be in Dale's arms, or maybe even his bedroom, albeit in a hotel room.

Dale offered to drive Armani home, but she declined the favor. Dale's next move was to invite her to meet him at a nearby upscale restaurant for dinner in an hour. Armani agreed, her mind already going to her closet and mentally choosing what she would wear. Armani took a cab home, while Dale got his car from the valet.

As soon as the cab stopped at Armani's residence, she jumped out and had the cab fare and tip ready. She rushed into the building, bypassing the mailroom, and heading straight for her condo. She had sensed how horny Dale was, and she was feeling pretty passionate herself. She needed to slip into something very sexy, drive to the restaurant in her black *Porsche 911*, and make an entrance that would make all heads turn as she approached Dale's table. It was understood that Dale would arrive first.

Armani achieved the full effect, giving a flip of her long hair and a smile that let everyone know that what she was wearing was nothing special — just something she pulled out of her closet to cover her body. Well, it definitely covered her body! She wore a skin-tight, red leather jumpsuit with high heels to match the suit, and a brightly colored scarf around her neck instead of a blouse. Thus, her arms and much of her breasts were exposed. She changed her lipstick, too, so she looked like a model with everything matching well.

Armani didn't stop to ponder the fact that Dale was married, and that she had seen his wife, Katherine on several occasions. No, she was in the mood for a good screw, and she felt that somewhere in the future, she could use this Dale Clyburn in some way professionally. Armani always had an ulterior motive, even in the most intimate setting. The options seemed limitless, as she slowly walked up to Dale and gave him a playful peck on the cheek before taking her seat across from him. Armani and Dale were free to flirt as much as they liked because none of their common associates were dining there tonight.

While they perused the menu, Dale told Armani in a whisper that she was sexy, but he quickly followed that flattery with a question about what made her such a "hard ass." He also told her he liked her feistiness, after which she felt comfortable enough to tell him much of the story about what happened between her ex-husband and her.

While Dale acted like he was listening attentively to every word Armani uttered, he was thinking nasty thoughts about her. Dale saw how vulnerable she was while talking about her ex-, so he seized the moment and licked his lips slowly, making sure Armani noticed. As she stopped talking and focused on his mouth, he moved his lips to silently let her know he wanted her.

Armani wanted him too, so she invited Dale to her condo since there were a number of judges and lawyers in the building that he could have been visiting. After a delicious dinner and a few glasses of wine, they agreed that Armani would get home first and alone, after which Dale would arrive at her building to visit "someone."

The couple left separately, and Armani hurried home to change clothes. Then she put a blue light bulb in one of her lamps, lit some incense, and put on her favorite music. Once Dale arrived, she offered him a drink, but he declined saying he only wanted her. Dale walked into her living room and loved the ambience. She had impeccable taste, which was a secondary turn-on for Dale.

Without warning, he took her hands and then moved his hands up her arms until he had her whole upper body in his strong hands. He pulled her towards him with an aggressive move, and she let out a barely audible squeal as she allowed herself to fall into his arms. He couldn't keep his hands off Armani, grabbing and kissing her. She was inebriated from the drinks at the restaurant, but she still had the presence of mind to think of ways she could use "Dale's ass" in a business setting. At that moment, however, all she wanted was Dale's ass – literally!

The foreplay was incredible and she had to hand it him -- the man knew how to use his tongue. He took all her clothes off slowly, tossing each piece onto the couch. He licked her body all over, and while he didn't rush to penetrate her, he really wanted to satisfy her and he did. She reciprocated licking his ears, then sucking his nipples, and before she knew it, he had a climax without them having intercourse.

Dale told Armani, who was nearly naked at this point, that she was delicious. They sat up talking a little, before he started kissing her around her navel. She leaned back on her elbows as if to give permission for more oral sex because she could handle a second orgasm within a half hour period.

Something crossed her mind, though, that changed her mood in an instant. She stopped him before he went any further, asking him why he was cheating on his wife. The mood changed immediately, as Dale straightened up and grabbed his undershirt. He didn't need to put it on right then, but he did need time to think of the right answer. So he was silent until his shirt was back on him. He told her his marriage to Katherine was one of convenience and not love.

He volunteered that Katherine loved him a lot, and that she would do anything to keep their marriage together. In her own right, she was strong, like the rest of her royal English family. But when she was home with Dale, all she wanted was to be in his arms. He admitted to Armani that when he first met Katherine, he had an amazing physical attraction to her, and he thought he wanted to marry her. However within the first couple of years, he realized she wasn't his "true love." As long as he didn't look directly into her eyes when he told his lies, he felt little remorse.

Armani was connecting with Katherine, thinking about her own husband and his need to find love outside of their marriage. It made her feel guilty about what they were doing, and she told Dale she had a conscience. She reached for her silk robe and tied it tightly around her waist. That was a signal that there would be no more sex that night and maybe never again. She politely asked him to leave, but Dale was getting ready for "round two," telling her every time he saw her in court, he wanted her and he would do whatever it took to have her in his life.

Armani realized in an instant how circumstance dictates who will cheat and when, and she and Dale had willingly cheated on Dale's wife. Just because Armani was single at the time didn't make her feel less guilty about having just had oral sex with someone with whom she would likely interact in the legal system many times in the future. She had made a mistake, and wanted to fix it.

Finally, Armani thought it best to describe what just happened that evening as a "one-night-stand" and they were done. Dale's ego was crushed, but he got dressed quickly and left. Dale wasn't sure he wanted to pursue Armani further, despite being physically attracted to her. His ego was very important to him, and he wasn't used to rejection. In fact, none of the other women with whom he cheated on Katherine had rejected him. They all wanted a relationship with Dale, but he considered them a one-night-stand. Wow, it hurts when "the shoe is on the other foot!"

Armani sat silently in her living room, thinking hard about Dale. She still wanted him, and she really wanted more of his touch when making love. He had hit all the pleasure points on her body, and she was still tingling all over.

But she chastised herself out loud as she walked into her bathroom to take a cold shower before going to bed. She decided before getting under her covers that she would never mess around with another married man. It wasn't worth trying to get even with her own ex- because she couldn't stop thinking about Dale now. She hadn't counted on him staying in her head like this. She tossed and turned half the night before finally drifting off into a deep state of relaxation.

Chapter 5
Keo Staffort

Keo Staffort owned a very successful, small technology company that kept him quite busy. Still, he made time to follow his passion by traveling to the west coast bi-weekly to sing in his brother's band.

Keo lived in a quaint section of Philadelphia called *Society Hill*, that's close to restaurants and fun nightlife. It was also close to 1400 South, the glamorous and expensive high-rise building where Armani Johnson lived. Keo was born in Ocho Rios, Jamaica and lived there until he was sixteen years old.

Then his parents moved Keo and his younger brother to Philadelphia. His father got a job working for an NFL team, since he was an ex-football player who suffered an injury that destroyed his football career, but he wanted to remain in the sports world. When he got the call to be an assistant general manager, he relocated the family to Philly.

Keo loved football but had no interest in playing it because his first love was technology and tinkering with computers. He respected his father's love for the game, and supported his vision when they moved to Piladelphia so his Dad could work with the NFL. Keo grew up as what we would call a "geek," loving solitude and gadgets more than bouncing balls and running hard with the kids in his neighborhood.

Although considered a "brain" by his peers, Keo was also very handsome. He looked a little like the actor Idris Elba. Keo got good grades throughout school, and upon graduation from high school he attended *Drexel University* and majored in Computer Science. He became a "genius" software developer who could rebuild computers and sell them to family and friends. He was an expert when it came to game programming and development, too.

However, Keo was also a talented singer, which few people knew about. He hung out with a local band, singing backup sometimes, and he even toured with them when he wasn't traveling west to sing with his brother, or making money from his talent as a computer software developer. He never fashioned himself to be a solo artist on stage, with female fans throwing their lace panties at him. But he felt pretty good about being the background to the one who enjoyed being center stage.

Well, Keo did OK performing locally with his small band, but what he really enjoyed was being part of his brother's band out in California. He considered that "the big leagues," compared to the "small potatoes" of his local band. Still, making music was music to Keo's ears, and he loved it all!

Maybe it was because Keo's professional job was so intellectually focused that he relished those times when he flew to the West Coast to relax and enjoy the music he helped to create with his brother's band. Naturally, it was always good to see family, too. His brother's group sang *Motown* oldies, which was the favorite of every member of the band.

Most of the guys were between thirty and forty-five years old, so they were past the age of ogling young women while they performed. When they rehearsed, there was a lot of laughing, eating and cussing going on in the studio. The musicians spent a lot of time at a Producer's home studio since it had all the state-of-the-art equipment that Keo was instrumental in setting up. His brother was a great dancer, so he was the choreographer and the baby of the group.

Keo flew between the East and West Coast as often as his tech job would permit, and on those long trips, he always reflected on what life would be like with Armani. Whenever his California group sang the slow, soulful ballads, Keo's thoughts would go to her. As much as he flirted with other women, his heart was with her but he knew she didn't feel the same way about him.

He fantasized about how and when she would run towards him in slow motion, like women did in those romantic commercials. He craved the day when Armani would run into his arms and allow him to caress her tenderly. But until then, he would do what men did – charm all the ladies and bed as many as he could!

Perhaps the most notable thing about Keo Staffort was his reputation for juggling his many women the way one would juggle balls in the air without letting one fall to the ground. He tried hard not to be alone because he enjoyed the company of women – fit and toned women who look good on his arm. At the same time, Keo was thinking that Armani Johnson was the "right one" for him. He always said he would be a bachelor the rest of his life if he didn't find anyone out there who could meet his high standards of having beauty and brains. Armani certainly met those standards!

Keo did treat his women well, and spoiled them all with fancy gifts and sweet gestures. In exchange, he felt it only fair that his women let him do whatever he wanted with his time away from them, without pressuring him to be tied down in one relationship. That's part of the reason he had the luxury of traveling between the East and West Coast as often as he did.

His personal challenge in balancing the life of a computer wizard and a wanna-be rock star backup singer was to remember not to cuss when he was dealing with clients or peers, and to cuss profusely when he was with his "boys." Sometimes those foul words fit, like at the last concert he played, where a woman stood right beneath him, picked up her short skirt, and took off her red lace thong. She balled it up and threw it on stage with phone number attached.

Keo caught the thong in mid-air, just as another musician reached for it. He heard himself say out loud, *"Who the fuck owns this? Red is my favorite color because it always makes my dick hard. So I want to fuck you if you got the courage to come on stage now."* She did!

When Keo Staffort first took a long look at Armani Johnson, he approached her the same way he approached all his women. He had a number of smooth, convincing one-liners that all his women found appealing. But he met his match with this strong-willed, attractive woman who filtered everything about her personal relationships through the lens of being a divorce lawyer.

She was hard to know and hard to please. Perhaps it was the "chase," or running after "forbidden fruit" that first caused Keo to pay extra attention to Armani. But it didn't take long for him to realize he truly had feelings for her, and could see himself becoming monogamous for the first time in his life.

Keo and Armani had first met at the gym across the street from 1400 South, which was much larger than the gym in Armani's building. So she often came to this gym to work out, and she developed a talent for weightlifting. Keo developed a talent for watching Armani out of the corner of his eye, while he was bench pressing weights and working on machines.

Keo was into physical fitness, so he frequented the gym several times a week when he was in town. He often saw Armani there, but the two just made small talk. However, after several months, Keo paid more attention to Armani's changing body. She was, in fact, becoming more toned and shapely, and she already had a great body to begin with. Keo was trying to figure out the best way to get this lovely lady to talk to him.

He admired Armani's weight lifting skills, and one day, he walked right up to her while she was lifting, and asked how many pounds she could bench press. Armani smiled because she knew she was so good that she could lift 140 pounds easily. She added a little weight to the total weight she could comfortably press, knowing that Keo would never ask her to press weights to impress him. Armani called her little exaggeration a "white lie."

Armani had checked Keo out, off and on during the past year, and she admired his physique from a distance. She had a mindset not to get involved with any men after her ugly divorce. And then she found herself attracted to the man to whom she gave the code name "Mr. Prosecutor."

It was Dale Clyburn. She thought she might be in love with him! So why was she flirting with Keo Staffort? "What's wrong with me," Armani thought to herself. She couldn't help herself from beginning a relationship with Keo that could turn intimate, even though she had once been intimate with Dale.

Armani often spotted Keo while he was lifting, and she quietly wondered what it would be like to have intercourse with this good-looking man with a fit body. Seems they communicated without words because both

Armani and Keo started coming to the gym more often, and each worked out a little harder to impress the other. Did we have a gender competition going here?

After just two months, they started working out almost everyday, and naturally, a friendship formed. Keo realized this woman could potentially make him turn his life around for the better. He told himself, *"Hey, I've been looking for that special woman to tame my wild side, but I don't know if I'm ready to commit to having my sharp teeth filed down to a normal size. I might lose my edge for biting."* Hmmm....what a dilemma for Keo to have! And yet, instead of running far from Armani Johnson, Keo was drawn especially close to her.

Keo had one big problem, as he assessed what *he* was willing to do to change his life. He accepted the fact that he had deep feelings for Armani, but recognized that right now, she didn't feel the same way about him. He needed to strike a delicate balance between trying to act like they were just friends, while at the same time taking advantage of every opportunity to seduce her into being his woman. Yes, he had to admit that he was willing to give up all his other women for this one!

Keo returned home from a trip to San Francisco, where he had big fun playing those *Motown* tunes with his brother's band. The woman with the red lace thong went home with Keo after the concert, and she exposed him to some West Coast freaky sex.

He was in an especially good mood, as he prepared his mind for his career job responsibilities. He put down his luggage, and as he went to the refrigerator for something cold to drink, a slew of cuss words exited from his mouth because the frige was empty.

He checked his messages and saw that Armani had left a voice mail asking him to attend Happy Hour with her at 1400 South. Armani wanted him to go with her in case it was boring that night. She would have an excuse to say they had plans for the evening, but were just stopping by to say *"Hello."* Keo was tired, but he returned her call and told her he would regroup and see her at 7:00 pm.

Even though he had secret, deep feelings for Armani, he liked the fact that coming to her classy building meant the possibility of him scoring a piece of ass with any number of attractive women. Besides, he was tired of "yanking his crank" while thinking about "Ms. Red Thong" since he got home.

Keo had time for a quick nap, shit, shower and shave. He was getting excited thinking about the possibilities of women who would be in attendance at Happy Hour. He'd been to Armani's building before, and had seen the caliber of the women residents, and even the invited female guests of the women residents. Keo liked what he saw. Mind you, Keo wasn't conceited, although he knew he was a handsome specimen of a man with a milk chocolate complexion and a great body.

Still, he was definitely "eye candy" and he knew it. He liked attending social events with Armani, since she was attractive and sexy, and he was the envy of the other men checking her out, since people always assumed they were a couple. In truth, after months of making general conversation at the gym across the street from 1400 South, they had become good friends, and Keo knew he had to settle for the friend relationship until he could find a way to begin a romantic relationship with Armani.

There wasn't anything he wouldn't do for her, and they talked about everything because they were so comfortable and trusting of each other. She never judged him, and she even double-dated with him in the past. They had a great friendship, but deep down inside, Keo felt more sure by the day that she was the one for him. Until that happy day came, however, he would continue to "play the field."

Keo hopped in a cab and it took fifteen minutes to get to 1400 South. Armani met him in the lobby and they headed to where Happy Hour was underway, with a few people already mingling. Armani introduced Keo and made sure she told everyone they were good friends. They were together for a short time, but then Armani separated from him once she saw him flirting with a woman she knew named "Mercedes." She recognized a couple of lawyers, so she went over to speak with them.

Meanwhile, Keo engaged in a light conversation with Mercedes, which seemed to have lasted the whole evening. Armani glanced in his direction a few times, but he was engrossed in conversation. Armani surmised that Keo might leave at the end of the evening with Mercedes, but it was none of her business. She intended to go to her unit, maybe have one more glass of wine and listen to her music before going to bed alone.

Keo, on the other hand, had no intentions of going to bed alone. He was enchanted with this lovely lady named

Mercedes Johannson. She was gorgeous, with tiny freckles on her face that made her look just a little "devilish."

She was taller than most women, standing at 5'11" and weighing about 135 pounds. She was muscular in all the right places, but soft around the bosom, neck and cheeks. Keo thought she reminded him a little of Kimora Lee Simmons, wife of the famous rap promoter and media mogul Russell Simmons. She knew how to flirt, and Keo Stafford was a pro at receiving it.

"So, you have an interesting name, Mercedes Johannson. I know your ancestry can't be Scandinavian or Swedish because you're sporting an old-fashioned 'Afro,' and your eyes look slightly Asian. Where'd your name come from?" Mercedes answered that she was of mixed heritage, with her mother being Japanese and her father African-American.

Her countenance fell very briefly, as she explained that her father was absent from the home after her mother died in childbirth, delivering Mercedes. An aunt raised her in a home without much affection and praise. So her personality was shaped by a childhood where her needs were adequately provided for, but her desire to give and receive affection was non-existent.

Mercedes lightened the conversation by saying her last name was, in fact, Swedish, because her Dad's ancestors lived on a plantation owned by Master Sven Johannson. Keo gave out a laugh at that name, but nodded to show he understood that most African-Americans have last names that can be traced back to slave owners. She didn't offer her birth name, but quickly added that she changed her name to "Mercedes" on her 21st birthday. She spelled it just like the expensive car she always admired, and it made her intriguing to men like Keo Staffort. Keo took a sip of his drink and then said, *"I'll bet you're high maintenance, just like the car, too."* Mercedes flashed a wide grin in agreement, but made no comment.

Keo noticed how perfect and white her teeth were. Her lips were full and naturally pink, and the reason he noticed that was her lipstick was almost gone when she finished her first drink. His eyes moved from her face to her nicely shaped legs and black high heels. Before he allowed himself to focus on her crotch, he purposely made eye contact again – and quickly! His unclean thoughts might have been, *"This Mercedes might be a good fuck, but I wouldn't want a lasting relationship with her shallow ass."*

Mercedes volunteered that she was a flight attendant working for a major airline for the past several years. She valued her career above relationships with men, but hid that fact from Keo because she also loved sex and saw this handsome man as someone with whom she might enjoy a one-night stand.

She placed her small hand inside of Keo's bigger hand, pointing out the contrast between her fair, smooth skin and his dark, beautiful skin. Mercedes was the complexion of her mother, though she got her hair texture from her father.

The whole time Mercedes was going on and on about herself, Keo pretended to listen intently to her every word. He had mastered the art of pretending to listen, while allowing his eyes to discretely wander around a crowded room, just in case another fine woman was looking in his direction. Sure enough, he spotted a woman with a completely different look from that of Mercedes, but equally attractive.

Keo saw the woman heading for the bar, and asked Mercedes if she wanted another drink. She didn't but he excused himself anyway, saying he would be right back. He gave one quick, hard glance around the entire room as he walked slowly to the bar. He was looking to see where Armani was. He saw her laughing with some friends, gave a little sigh because he longed to be with her someday, and then reached the bar, right where this fine lady was standing.

Keo was smooth, and he knew it. He pretended to order a drink, in case Mercedes was looking. But he introduced himself to the woman, whose name was Tiffany O'Brien. She asked if he lived in the building, to which he responded that he lived in *Society Hill*, but had come to Happy Hour as the guest of Armani Johnson. Tiffany immediately asked if Armani was Keo's "lady," but Keo quickly shut down any thoughts like that by saying they were just friends.

Keo spotted Mercedes heading towards him, probably because she noticed him standing too close to another woman, and she intended to leave with Keo Staffort! So he got the bartender's attention and ordered a drink. The two women eyed each other the way women do when they are both flirting with the same man. Keo tried awkwardly to introduce one to the other, but Tiffany said they knew each other because they both lived at 1400 South. They weren't close friends, but had certainly seen each other at Happy Hour and in the mailroom pretty regularly. *"Oh, well.....then you ladies don't need me to make introductions."*

Just then, the bartender handed Keo his drink, and he put it to his mouth so quickly that he almost slurped the liquid. He had said quite enough for that moment. Tiffany attempted to flirt with Keo, but before she could say much, Mercedes positioned herself between them and placed her arm in Keo's to signal that they were a couple, if only for that evening. She gave a plastic smile to Tiffany. *"I'm sure I'll see you around here coming and going, and it's so good that we've bumped into each other at Happy Hour. Keo, I left my drink on the table where we were sitting, so let's finish our conversation over there. The bar area is so crowded, don't you think?"*

Tiffany got the strong hint, and while she would like to have said more to Keo, she was a professional woman who would never make a scene – especially over a man! As Mercedes gently escorted Keo back to where they had been sitting and talking most of the evening, he told himself that he could do worse than "settling" for a night with this woman. He could also go home alone.

Keo was used to talking to himself, responding to himself, and still holding a conversation with another person. Mercedes was more absorbed in herself than anyone else, but felt the need to ask some cursory questions about Keo's life. Her motive was to find a mutual topic of conversation in which they would engage, as they left Happy Hour together.

Armani Johnson had left Happy Hour while all this was going on, wishing to enjoy the privacy and solitude of her condo while listening to her favorite music. Keo and Mercedes looked around, just in case any of the residents at 1400 South were staring at them. Neither of them wanted to be the subject of the next morning's gossip. Tiffany O'Brien had apparently either gone to the bathroom or left Happy Hour altogether, so not a single person was staring at Keo and Mercedes. Everyone was busy socializing and drinking. Some hoped to enjoy the "under covers" company of residents or guests who attended this month's Happy Hour.

Keo whispered some words into Mercedes' ear, and then gently kissed the ear. He softly bit her earlobe to indicate that if she left with him, he would pleasure her all night. She understood his unspoken language and leaned in towards him, as her passion rose within her. Keo took Mercedes by the arm, and led her outside, where they took a cab to his place, and spent the night together.

As soon as they closed the door to his townhouse, Mercedes began undressing Keo. She had aggressive fingers, and he liked the rough treatment. They moved as if waltzing to the couch, where Mercedes threw Keo down. Her purse was still attached to her shoulder, and with one hand continually rubbing Keo's groin area, she pulled out handcuffs and a small whip with her other hand. The purse fell to the floor, with a single tube of lipstick falling out.

Keo had never experienced bondage before, but he had no problems being in tutelage under this masterful woman's touch. She glanced wildly around the living room, spotting one straight back chair with tall arms. Without warning, she had lifted Keo by his unbuttoned shirt to a standing position, and gently pulled him to the chair. He sat down heavily.

Mercedes put the whip in her teeth, and handcuffed Keo to the chair. Both of them were breathing heavily. Somehow, he had lost his trousers in the movement from the couch to the chair, and she had lost all her clothes from the waist down.

Mercedes asked Keo if a woman had ever whipped him before, and he weakly said *"No."* She said, *"You're in for a special treat, so close your eyes!"* Keo obeyed, having neither the ability nor the will to be released from those tight cuffs.

The next morning, they parted early because each had things to do. Mercedes had the next few days off, and planned to do some grocery shopping before going home. While riding in the cab back to her residence, she hummed the tune to the *Pointer Sisters'* song about *"a man with a slow hand."* The cab driver chimed in because he remembered the words Mercedes couldn't. She got a double chuckle out of that!

In Mercedes' head, she felt she had made a love connection with Keo, since they had enjoyed Happy Hour and then spent an incredibly satisfying night together. She was thinking about her past relationships and how she never wanted a commitment before. Part of the reason she avoided long-term relationships with men was that she tended to be too possessive and jealous. Rather than to risk driving them away and leaving her alone and bitter, Mercedes ended things on her terms. She protected her heart that way.

Last night was different. Mercedes felt something deep inside herself that had been buried for a long time. Now she speculated that Keo Staffort could be the one for her. She falsely assumed he felt the same way, but she was only musing to herself while riding in the cab going home. Mercedes told herself that her life was about to take a dramatic and very happy turn!

Chapter 6
Mercedes Johannson's "True Colors"

Mercedes Johannson was a strong-willed woman who didn't like being told what to do. She was very opinionated and thought she knew it all, which was an unflattering skill set she possessed that she could hide until she got to know a person. Especially when in the company of the opposite sex, Mercedes knew how to use her feminine charm to get what she wanted. Once she was comfortable, however, she couldn't help but show that bossy, opinionated, almost prejudicial side of her.

She was beautiful and very exotic looking, since her mother was Japanese and her father was African-American. When she walked in a room, all eyes were on her big, curly, jet-black Afro because few women today sported the Angela Davis-style from the militant 1960s. Mercedes' eyes were slightly slanted, and she had the fine, almost angular facial features of her mother.

Because she looked a little like Kimora Lee Simmons, ex-wife of entrepreneur giant, Russell Simmons, people were always asking her if she were a model, but she always smiled and said she was "just" a flight attendant for one of the largest airlines.

She had worked for several airlines over fifteen years, and dated an array of fine men from pilots to celebrities she had met on the plane. However, the relationships never lasted because, just when a wonderful man was interested in establishing a deeper relationship with Mercedes, she ended what she considered to be an affair.

She always made sure her men realized the number of hours and days flight attendants were away from their families, which was her way of letting these man down easily. She proudly acknowledged that she was career-minded, looking to advance and not settle down. That implied that she wasn't interested in having kids, either. Maybe this goes back to her childhood, which was missing much genuine affection.

Mercedes was raised by an aunt on her father's side after her mother died from complications delivering her. Her father was a career man in the military who traveled all over the world. He would send money to her aunt every month for Mercedes' wellbeing. Although her aunt always stressed academic achievement as the way to get ahead, she didn't give Mercedes the physical or emotional "fluff" that most young girls craved. Her aunt lived in the Strawberry Mansion neighborhood of Philadelphia. The name of the section where she grew up sounded like there were mansions lined up along the street, but it was a working class neighborhood.

She had great neighbors who looked out for each other, and she even rode to school with a neighbor who taught at her school, *Girls' High*. She didn't like attending an all-girls school, but it was for smart girls and she was very intelligent. The boys around her previous, public school were starting to notice her and she them, so her aunt enrolled her in the all-girls' school, hoping she would concentrate on her studies to be a doctor or lawyer. Initially, Mercedes followed her aunt's guidance and studied hard because she intended to be a doctor or lawyer.

However, after her first trip on an airplane, Mercedes abandoned what she thought were her future plans, but which were really the dreams of her aunt who never had the opportunities afforded Mercedes. She fell in love with flying, particularly what she perceived to be the glamorous things the stewardess did.

On a trip with her father to Disneyland in California, she made the decision in her mind that being an airline stewardess would fulfill her dreams that were so much larger than the neighborhood where she grew up. After graduating from high school, she filled out applications with all the airlines, and one of the largest called her in for an interview. Mercedes was charming, as well as good-looking. Her mixed heritage served her well because she stood apart from the dozens of young women looking to join the airlines. So naturally, Mercedes Johannson became a flight attendant, exiting the flight attendant school program with excellent scores.

Mercedes was a successful and popular flight attendant for fifteen years, during which time she has traveled the world. She served the needs of countless passengers, graciously diffused tensions that certain passengers brought on board the plane, and pleased her superiors with her consistent performance. She still loved her job after all those years.

She lived at 1400 South in a two-bedroom condominium, and chose the location because of its proximity to downtown and the airport. She had been thinking it might be time to settle down, but with whom? The prospect of a romantic relationship after years of putting men off was more than Mercedes wanted to think about at that time. She had just returned home after a long flight overseas and she was exhausted. She wanted to get home and relax, since she would be off the next four days.

She went into the mailroom to grab her mail before getting on the elevator, but had to stop at the front lobby to sign for some packages that had come while she was away. Once she got on the elevator, she noticed the sign posted about Happy Hour. She thought about it for a second, not committing one way or another since she was bogged down with her luggage, mail, and packages. She always enjoyed Happy Hour, but right now, all she wanted to do was get inside her unit.

Once inside she took off her coat, shoes and jewelry. She decided not to unpack, but took a shower after putting her luggage on the balcony as she always did, fearful that some insects or critters may be in her luggage from all that traveling. She usually left her baggage on the balcony until the next day, and then unpacked. Mercedes decided to order a pizza and watch some television while opening her mail. She thought about Happy Hour and decided she would go after all, since it was the next evening. She was dog-tired and fell asleep with unopened mail strewn around her bed. When she awoke, she couldn't believe it was the next morning.

She wasn't hungry, but had a glass of orange juice and ate an apple that was in the refrigerator. She knew she had to go food shopping, since she loved fresh fruits and vegetables but had neither in the house. Because of her rigorous travel schedule, Mercedes usually purchased just enough for the time she expected to be in town. She finished what little mail was left to open, separated her bills from the junk mail, and thought she would write some checks and pay her bills. After all of that, she would figure out what she was wearing to Happy Hour.

She had so many clothes and shoes in her closet from which to choose something sexy to wear. After trying on a few outfits and smiling at herself in the full-length mirror in her bedroom, she chose a black mini dress with a cut out in the back that showed skin. She had a black pair of suede ankle booties with a high heel, and completed her ensemble with some exquisite gold jewelry from St. Thomas, where she purchased something every time she worked a flight going there.

Mercedes took one last look at herself in the mirror and smiled as she picked the Afro to be sure it was as full as possible. She liked the fact that she had fine Japanese features, but could sport a big Afro on her head that made people stare in confusion about what exactly her heritage consisted of. She arrived the same time as one of the other residents who was gorgeous, but the women didn't know each other.

Mercedes wanted to make the solo grand entrance so all eyes would be on her, but now here was this woman whom she had to admit was a beauty arriving the same time as she did. Someone kissed the woman's hand and said something like, *"Welcome, Miss Dior."* Mercedes gave her a hard, cold stare as she stepped up her pace just enough to enter the Happy Hour lounge half a foot ahead of Miss Dior.

As soon as Mercedes walked into the Happy Hour lounge, she saw a handsome man who caught her eye, and she couldn't stop looking at him. He was eyeing her and she couldn't help but introduce herself to him, asking if he lived in the building. He told her his name was Keo Staffort and he lived in *Society Hill*, but was invited by his good friend, Armani Johnson, whom he pointed out to Mercedes. Armani was standing with some lawyer friends across the room, not noticing Keo pointing her out to Mercedes.

Mercedes didn't know her, but had seen her in the mailroom from time to time. She turned her full attention to Keo Staffort, thinking herself to be so fine that she could get any man anytime. She came to Happy Hour looking to see whom she could get to kiss her ass by the end of the evening – literally! Mercedes felt a strong physical attraction to Keo, quietly feeling like this man was hers, and she wasn't willing to share him.

Her attitude towards all men changed in an instant because with Keo, it was love at first sight. She didn't care if Keo felt the same about her because she would make it her personal mission to cause him to think as she did – he must look at her and think he's found love at first sight.

Keo asked if she wanted a drink, and they walked to the bar together, where she ordered a glass of champagne. They left the bar and found two seats near some other residents whom Mercedes ignored because she was laughing and giggling at everything this handsome man said. She didn't know if it was the champagne or if he was that funny, but she couldn't stop giggling like a schoolgirl.

During the time the couple stayed at Happy Hour, some of the other women tried introducing themselves to the handsome man who didn't live at 1400 South. However, Mercedes knew how to distract Keo from interacting with anyone besides her. There was one woman named "Tiffany," who tried more than once to get Keo's attention.

Mercedes considered her a pain in the ass for interrupting their conversation just to talk about something unimportant. Although Tiffany tried once more to position herself next to Keo, she was no match for Mercedes, who could nudge another woman out of her sphere of social influence with the skill of a greedy kitten pushing its tiny siblings away from getting their mother's milk.

While Keo was planning to get Mercedes to leave with him, hoping they could spend another kinky night together, Mercedes was feeling a little tired, but wasn't about to leave him there talking to Tiffany. She thought she met the man of her dreams, and she intended for this night to end with Keo Staffort holding her in his arms as the sun came up. But with Tiffany drooling all over him, Mercedes weakened briefly by thinking that seriously dating a brainiac software developer might be a bigger mental challenge than she cared to handle.

It's interesting that Mercedes had Keo's full attention, and yet when she saw this other attractive woman falling all over him she assumed his head could be turned from looking at her to looking at Tiffany. In reality, all Keo wanted that night was Mercedes!

Just as Mercedes was about to go into the dark place in her mind, where she found reasons not to leave with Keo or any man, Keo gently took her arm, and ushered her out of the building to find a cab. He intended to "score," and didn't want midnight to come while he was still on "first base." Poor Tiffany was disappointed because she was left standing at the bar at Happy Hour, either looking foolish or looking to find someone with whom to spend the night. It was certain not to be Keo!

The next day Mercedes was on her way grocery shopping, when Armani got on the elevator. Both women gave the polite smile we all use when we're on a quiet elevator. Mercedes was thinking, *"I shouldn't say anything to her stuck-up ass,* but after all, she is Keo's friend, so maybe she can tell me something important about him. In her mind, she was thinking, *"Those two probably had an affair and now they're just friends. Who in the hell are they fooling?"*

She did manage to say, *"Hi Armani, how are you?"* Armani gave her a fake smile and a weak hello, but no more words were spoken before Armani got off the elevator. Mercedes regretted saying anything to her, and her gut was telling her to leave Keo alone. But her emotions were telling her they had a love connection. She got into the store and bought the few things on her shopping list. She was thinking about making a meatloaf and baked sweet potato for dinner, so she bought the ingredients for that and picked up a *Sara Lee* pound cake to satisfy her sweet tooth.

Mercedes was leaving the store when she bumped into Tiffany O'Brien, the resident she had met at Happy Hour. It seemed like every time she was in the grocery store, there was a resident or two in there. Tiffany gave her a grudging salutation.

When Mercedes got home with her groceries, she was hoping Keo would call her before he left to go out of town. She was off for four days, and hoped they could spend at least one more night during that time. She was not one to make the first call after spending the night with someone, but it was bugging her. So she called Keo and was surprised by his sort of cold tone when he answered the phone. She started off in her sweet voice, telling him she enjoyed the night before and was looking forward to seeing him again very soon. She didn't suggest seeing him *that* day, but was hoping he would get the hint.

Instead, he told her he had plans and would be busy the next couple of days before he hit the road. She was very disappointed and wondered what happened since she saw him the night before, because she thought for sure they had a love connection. They hung up and she sat in her living room dumbfounded, thinking it must be that bitch, Tiffany, who got to him. Mercedes had an insanely jealous personality, and though she tried hard to keep it from surfacing while she did her job as a top-notch flight attendant with a reputation for cordiality, that "green monster" was coming out of her with the hunger for vengeance displayed in the old movie *"Alien."*

Mercedes was going to get to the bottom of this, so she wrote Tiffany a note telling her she needed to speak with her ASAP, and stuck it in Tiffany's mailbox. Later that day, Mercedes got a call from her supervisor, asking if she would come to work and fill in for someone the next day. Although pissed off because she might have had other plans, she agreed to do it, since she had nothing else planned and didn't have to be at work until 1:00pm the next day. She had time to see Keo, if he would just call her back with that suggestion.

After having a conversation with herself about whether or not she would see Keo before she went to work the next afternoon, Mercedes figured she wouldn't be seeing Keo after his tone was so cold. Still, she felt she had a "Plan B," which was to speak with Armani, his "so called" friend. She was curious to find out more about Keo, since she wanted a romantic relationship with him. She was unsure if Tiffany or Armani had a previous or current relationship with Keo, so she decided to do some checking, just in case he was using her.

After all, Mercedes was proud of the fact that she used men and then discarded them because she was determined that no one would get close to her heart. Then, in an instant, Keo Staffort had her heart – all of it! She got out the *Residents Directory* and found Armani's unit number. She planned to stick a note under her door, asking Armani to call her. While leaving Armani's unit, Mercedes thought she should have put the note in her mailbox like she did with Tiffany.

Mercedes put away her groceries. The phone rang, and to her surprise, Armani had not only received and read her note, but also picked up the phone to call, as requested. The conversation didn't go well because Armani hung up on her. All she did was ask Armani questions about Keo, but this annoyed Armani. Armani told her to ask him whatever questions were on her mind because Armani was uncomfortable talking about Keo behind his back. Then she hung up the phone. Mercedes felt disappointment, but not defeat!

Mercedes was about to walk into the kitchen to make her meatloaf when Keo called her. Keo told her he was having a bad morning after getting some unpleasant news about work, and asked if she would like to have dinner with him. She said, *"Yes,"* but wondered what really happened. Then she thought about the note she stuck in Tiffany's mailbox asking her to call her. Now, she had to come up with an excuse as to why she wanted to speak with her. She thought she would ask her if she wanted to do some sightseeing and have a girl's day, even though Mercedes really wasn't interested in sightseeing with Tiffany.

Mercedes had to regroup for a second, speculating about what made him change his mind about seeing her. Was he really having a bad morning or did Tiffany tell him she wasn't interested in him, and he needed someone to rebound to? If that were true, Keo didn't understand that Mercedes Johannson was not the type to take second place for any man. She hadn't asked him where they were dining, but she was going to dress sexy so his eyes would be all over her. She decided she wouldn't "give up anything" tonight, but would tease him and make him squirm as he tried unsuccessfully to hide his erection.

A few minutes after she hung up with him, she finished making her meatloaf and put it in the refrigerator to cook later. She got excited walking to her bedroom, looking for something sexy in her wardrobe. The phone rang and it was Tiffany. They exchanged pleasantries and then Mercedes asked her if she wanted to go sightseeing the next weekend. Tiffany said, "Yes" so quickly because she had wanted someone to accompany her to visit the *Betsy Ross House, Fels Planetarium,* the *Art Museum* and any other place Mercedes felt they could see -- all in one day -- so they set the time and anticipated having a great time together.

However, just before hanging up, Mercedes made the tactical mistake of asking Tiffany if she had spoken much with Keo. Tiffany got an instant attitude with Mercedes, asking her where that question came from. She tried to remain a lady, but her mastery of foul language surfaced, and she heard herself say, *"It isn't any of your fucking business."* Now, Tiffany thought Mercedes had a motive for calling her, so she cut off the planned date and told Mercedes to kiss her ass. Then she hung up the phone by slamming it down on the receiver. Mercedes realized before the call was disconnected that she had overstepped her boundaries, but because her feelings for Keo were so strong, she forgave herself for all her actions the past twenty-four hours.

Mercedes planned to ask Keo what he knew about all this when she saw him next. When Keo asked if she'd like to go to

Warmdaddy's, she told him that was her favorite place and she'd meet him there at 7:30 p.m. They had live entertainment and you never knew who might stop by. There were numerous celebrities who ate there, and when Mercedes was in town, she looked forward to eating there.

She hopped in a cab and headed for *Warmdaddy's*. She wondered what was up with Keo, since one minute he was aloof, and the next, he was calling and asking her to dinner. Her feelings for him were starting to wane, and she didn't know if he was the one for her or not anymore. Tonight, she planned to be flirty.

Just like the night at Happy Hour, Mercedes knew she looked especially sexy and elegant. She had on black skinny jeans that fit her like a glove, a black silk low-cut top that showed her cleavage, and high heel ankle booties. She had on a cashmere coat that was ¾ inch length, and it was stunning. She knew she looked hot and it didn't take very long to get to the restaurant, so when she arrived, Keo had just arrived and was waiting to be seated. She got out the cab and walked slowly in the door thinking Keo was watching from inside. He was, and as she got closer, he opened the door for her from inside and gave her a hug as if they were a couple, telling her how great she looked.

Keo was "dressed to the nines," as they say, and he looked and smelled so good. He was wearing *Tom Ford* from top to bottom and he too, looked sexy. She started feeling something again for him but knew she would proceed with caution with him. They got seated and were making small "chit-chat." The waitress asked if she could get them a drink, and Mercedes wanted a gin and tonic. Keo ordered rum and Coke.

They hardly looked at the menu since both knew what they wanted, besides each other. She ordered the crab cakes and asparagus and he ordered the same, but with a side of mac and cheese. He told her he was glad to go out with someone who actually didn't just eat salads. Mercedes told him that when she was in town, she would always try and cook healthy meals because she ate so unhealthy while on the road or flying from place to place.

Their food came and she ate heartily. Mercedes could tell Keo was looking at her in that *certain* way, no doubt thinking he wasn't going to let her get away without having intercourse tonight. He saw her reaching down and taking off her ankle booties. The next thing he knew, she was running her bare foot up and down his leg, trying to get him going. She was doing a good job because both of them could feel his penis starting to get hard. Finally, she moved her seat from slightly across from him to right next to him.

Keo wondered what would happen next, but he figured anything that aroused this woman was good for Keo Staffort! Mercedes looked around discretely, until she was certain that their waiter was taking care of customers across the room. With a sexy, sadistic grin on her face, she put her hand under the table and started unzipping his fly and pulling out his penis. She was pulling on it with long strokes with one hand, and holding her fork with the other hand, as if ready to take the next bite of food. She never said a word, nor did she glance in his direction. Doesn't every normal woman discretely hold a penis in one hand and a fork in the other, while sitting in a semi-private booth in a crowded restaurant?

She was sitting there cool as a cucumber, and just as he was about to put his fork into his mac and cheese she pulled his penis so hard that he thought he was going to choke! Mercedes whispered, *I'll bet you like that and want more of it.* She hadn't changed her mind about going home alone even if she made herself so horny that she had to masturbate to fall asleep. No, this was a test to see what Keo thought of Mercedes Johannson the *person*. She was falling for him, and needed to know if all he saw in her was a sex object.

Keo was thinking one thing and Mercedes was thinking another. Yes, women and men think very differently when love and sex enter the relationship. Keo had to admit to himself that, as sex crazy as this bitch was, he never had anybody play with his penis like that. Matter of fact, he felt an unusually strong sensation because they were engaging in sexual foreplay right in plain sight of a restaurant full of people. No one noticed, which made his heart race and sweat begin to surface above his lips and around his collar. Still, he didn't want her to stop.

Keo could feel himself about to do something he would regret because he was noisy during lovemaking, so he quickly grabbed Mercedes' hand and stopped her increasingly rapid hand movements. *"Listen, we might need to take this to my place or yours, but we can't do any more here or I might scream out loud. Let's face it - I couldn't pretend I felt that much passion eating mac and cheese! Let's finish eating and leave this place."*

Mercedes gave a playful laugh at his last comment. She had Keo right where she wanted him. But that ugly jealousy surfaced, and she heard herself respond to Keo's sweet talk with, *"You know, honey, I need to ask you a question. Remember the woman who annoyed us at the bar during Happy Hour?"* Keo said, *"Tiffany....O'Brien, I think. What about her?"* She was careful with her next sentence, but didn't have the inner strength to say something simple like, *"Oh, nothing." "I thought you two might have gotten together and continued her conversation about serving on some board, or whatever she tried to bend your ear about at Happy Hour."*

Keo's whole countenance changed in an instant, and he looked at her before responding, *"Where the hell did that come from?"* He held back adding that if he did speak with her, it was none of Mercedes' fucking business. He saw her now as just another jealous chick, and he was thinking he didn't need that shit. They had enjoyed dinner up to that point, but Keo no longer wanted to bed her a second time. He had no idea she was in love with him, thinking they silently agreed to have sex without any strings attached.

"Maybe we should call it a night." He was pissed off and was hoping it didn't show, but she sensed his annoyance with her and it was getting late, so she put her ankle booties back on, and knew it was best if she went home without putting him through the test about his true feelings for her. Keo paid the check, and without more than a couple of words spoken between them, they left to go two separate ways. Being a gentleman, Keo hailed her a cab, and when it stopped, he surprised himself by jumping into it with her. What in the hell was he doing?

He told her he would ride with her to make sure she got home safe and sound. He had decided he wasn't going to mess with Mercedes again because he assessed that she had mental issues. Mercedes knew she had ruined the evening, and probably ruined any chances of being Keo's true love. She wanted to kick herself right in the ass, but that would have to wait until she was in the privacy of her home. She debated whether or not she should try to make up or just let it go. While all this conversation was going on in her head, the cab stopped because they were at 1400

South. She seemed startled because she had been lost in thought.

Once inside the building, she went to her condo and decided to pack her suitcase for an upcoming flight and forget about him. Instead of giving herself the promised tongue thrashing she deserved, Mercedes got into bed murmuring that he probably did find a way to connect with Tiffany. Maybe they both tried to spite her. As she closed her eyes, she uttered softly, *"I know I'm right. He was thinking about that bitch, Tiffany O'Brien, and I hate him. No, I hate her."* She cried into her pillow, and made an almost inaudible assessment of her predicament as she fell off to sleep. *"No, I hate me. I hate ME!"*

Chapter 7
Secrets and Lies

Pastor Elvis Paisley was a fine "man of the cloth" who had convinced his parishioners that "giving until it hurts" was their ticket to Heaven. He had a direct line to the Heavenly Father, so he often said, *"God spoke to me last night, and told me to tell His people to dig a little deeper and give according to the blessings each wanted God to bestow upon them. So if you want abundant blessings, you must give abundantly."* The congregation couldn't argue with that logic, especially since it came directly from the Lord Almighty!

In truth, Pastor Paisley was so dishonest that his wife left him after just three years of marriage. He would jump from one scheme to another, bringing some of his church members in on the scheme by duping them into believing he had an investment opportunity for them. No one ever made any money, except, of course, the shepherd of the flock.

The church was non-denominational, and Pastor Paisley originally attracted close to a hundred members. He preached powerful "fire and brimstone" sermons, warning parishioners to always seek to please God first and Pastor Elvis Paisley second. Old and young persons thought he was anointed to preach the true and living gospel, so they basically obeyed his requests for money and fasting and praying and more money, without question.

But after a while, congregants stopped coming because they were tired of feeling guilty for not surrendering their money for household bills to their spiritual leader. The messages from the pulpit became eerily similar, and less grounded in scriptures from the *Holy Bible*. The congregation had dwindled to about thirty loyal followers.

The church building was a small storefront on Broad Street in downtown Philadelphia, close to one of the hospitals. The church was opened everyday for anyone needing prayer. Pastor Elvis Paisley made sure a retired musician played the church organ softly in the background. He had learned in the Seminary, when he really sought the Lord "with all his heart and soul," that an effective way to reach sinners is through music that draws them into the church. From there, the pastor could appeal to their need for salvation, and bring them into the fold.

One day while Pastor Paisley was preparing for his Sunday sermon, a tall gentleman looking familiar walked in. Pastor greeted him and asked if he wanted to sit and pray alone, or if he wanted the pastor to pray with him. The gentleman introduced himself as Dale Clyburn, and Elvis Paisley knew in an instant that this was an attorney who had made the front page of the newspapers a few times.

Apparently, he won some high profile cases. Pastor Paisley regularly read about local celebrities, just in case there would be an opportunity for him to be in their company for reasons Paisley could create in a heartbeat. All he needed was opportunity – he already had motive, which was to funnel some funds from the wealthy to the "humble servant of God."

Dale had on an expensive suit, shoes and jewelry, and he seemed to have much on his mind. While Pastor Paisley was able to offer up a convincing prayer to God on behalf of Mr. Dale Clyburn, he was more interested in forming a relationship with this man who obviously had financial means. Surely there was a way these two honorable gentlemen could share the same cause.

Dale told Pastor he was going through some things involving his marriage, but didn't elect to go into details. Pastor Paisley gave Dale a sympathetic squeeze on his shoulder, but said to himself that he was fully aware that Dale was married to the daughter of a wealthy English Count. She had been in the newspapers for years because of her philanthropic deeds, and since Pastor made it a point to follow "lifestyles of the rich and famous," he had followed Miss Katherine Labelle Beaumont, even after she became Mrs. Dale Clyburn. Then, as Dale ascended in importance within his prestigious law firm, Pastor Paisley looked for news about either or both of them.

Pastor Paisley was almost drooling at the thought of getting some of the Beaumont and/or the Clyburn money, but he needed to be careful in his approach to these kinds of people. He pretended to know nothing about Dale's wife, but said only that relationships between men and women have been complicated since Eve convinced Adam to go against God's command and eat that forbidden fruit in the Garden of Eden.

Pastor Paisley sensed that Dale had a lot on his mind, so he stepped away briefly. Dale sat quietly in the church, contemplating whether or not to share the details of his failing marriage with this man. Katherine had been raised as a devout Catholic, and a divorce was considered a sin. It had taken Katherine Clyburn a long time and much soul-searching before she could even contemplate such an action against everything she believed in.

But Dale's persistent "womanizing" caused her more embarrassment than she deserved, and because she was a public figure too, she lacked the privacy to keep personal issues between herself and her husband. She had reached her limit, and so she sought the best divorce attorney in Philadelphia.

It was Armani Johnson "hands down." That's why she mustered the courage to call her, and she was a little confused when Armani suddenly ended their brief conversation, saying she would refer her to her assistant for an appointment. What Armani Johnson said to herself when she hung up the phone was really, *"I can't help HER!"*

Dale Clyburn decided he wasn't ready to volunteer the sordid details of his marital problems. He stood up, told Pastor Paisley that he had helped Dale to feel better. Pastor gave him an insincere smile and told him to stop by anytime. Dale left $300.00 in the offering box at the back of the church, and, as he exited the sanctuary, he told Pastor Paisley that if he ever needed anything to let him know.

Pastor Elvis Paisley was surprised, but pleased when he saw Dale Clyburn coming to Sunday service the next week. Dale continued to attend, and always left $300.00 in the offering plate. He always shook Pastor's hand after service and thanked him for his spiritual teachings. Other than that, Dale didn't join any church auxiliaries or attend Bible Study. Just church was enough for him. Perhaps he was building up the courage to share his marital problems with Pastor Paisley, or perhaps he was actually enjoying coming to church. Regardless of his reasons, he kept coming, and Pastor kept pondering how he could approach Dale to join him in a shady and dangerous endeavor. He had to be careful not to drive Dale away.

A few days after Dale had attended Pastor's church for a second month, Pastor was sitting at his desk after being served with divorce papers, and he wondered how he was going to maintain the church and pay his wife alimony. He told himself that his wife didn't value the covenant between a man and a woman, or she wouldn't ask him for a divorce.

He and his wife, along with the whole congregation, knew he was living a lie after one of the young, attractive congregants got pregnant with his baby. She was young and foolish enough to let church folks know that she was carrying Pastor Paisley's baby, and she was certain he would leave his wife for her. Pastor tried to restore the confidence the congregation had in him by offering this young woman money for an abortion. It never occurred to him that she might want to actually give birth to their "love child."

Pastor put his elbows on his desk, and then put his head in his hands, slowly shaking his head from side to side. He had made a mess of his life and his ministry, but this was no time for repentance. He needed money, and fast. Then he remembered that Dale

Clyburn said if he ever needed anything, he could come to Dale. It was time to tap into that generous offer, and time was of the essence for Pastor Elvis Paisley.

Pastor's demeanor changed and he regained his positive outlook. He and Dale Clyburn had in common the fact that both blatantly cheated on their spouses and both deserved the embarrassment of public divorces. They also had in common their respective desires to cover up their dirty deeds, rather than to "repent" and change their behavior. He would soon make his move to get close to Dale, and a social setting was perfect for men to let their guards down. Yep, Pastor Elvis Paisley saw a way to end his problems and save his reputation.

Pastor Paisley knew he was in BIG trouble when his wife told him she knew he had gotten a seventeen-year-old girl pregnant. Seems the girl's mother walked right up to Pastor's wife in church, and whispered that her daughter was pregnant and she was going straight to the police to report that their pastor had molested a minor child. She knew Pastor's wife would bring the news to him right away, and she waited for him to approach her with an offer to silence her.

The shame of it all was that Pastor Paisley had been grooming the young lady to be a Sunday school teacher for the young children who attended church, but were too fidgety to remain in the sanctuary during services. He knew this young girl had a crush on him, and he took advantage of that to "take her under his wing."

He said he was hoping to expand the church, and with more congregants coming, he wanted a separate place with a small classroom for the children. Naturally, this young girl would be his choice for the supervisor of the little kids. She glowed with excitement, assuring Pastor that she would not let him down. Shortly after that, Pastor let the girl down!

His wife begged the girl's mother not to go to the police, and though offering a bribe was against every one of her sensibilities, she swallowed her pride, hid her shock at this news, and calmly asked if the woman and her daughter would accept some financial aid if she were keeping the baby, or accept money for an abortion.

The mother told her she didn't believe in abortions and would help raise the baby. Therefore, she told the Pastor's wife, *"You tell* *that dirty hypocrite of a husband that I won't accept less than $25,000 'hush money' now, and once the baby's born, he WILL continue taking care of HIS child."* This woman was shrewd and knew she could always decide to go to the police because the law always protects minors.

Predictably, Pastor's wife was more than a little upset. First, she had to deal with her mate's betrayal, and after that face the fact that they didn't have the kind of money this mother was demanding. This was the last straw for his wife since she was tired of all the schemes she knew about, and had the instinct to realize he was hiding more wicked, mostly failed plots from her as well. She seriously contemplated the date she would leave her *"pastor,"* but staying in this marriage was not an option!

The next Sunday after church, Pastor approached Dale to ask if he would like to join him in watching a hockey game once in awhile. Dale thought it was a fine idea, and in his mind, he was already thinking he might tell Katherine he was going to his pastor's home for a game, after which he would meet a woman before going home. Or....Dale might *pretend* to be going to the home of his spiritual leader for a social gathering, but instead go straight to the arms and bed of some woman with whom he was cheating. To Dale, all the options gave him a "win-win." He agreed to come to Pastor's home the following Friday evening to watch a hockey game.

The two less than honorable men became friends who sometimes watched a hockey game at Pastor's home. Pastor's wife was always home and always hospitable to Dale. But Dale knew something was wrong between Pastor and his wife, because she was visibly cold towards her husband. He tried to cover it up by saying he was married to a moody woman who might be bi-polar – undiagnosed, of course!

By and by, Pastor Elvis Paisley opened up about his immediate problem of impregnating a young member of his congregation. He volunteered that, while the girl was naïve and wanted to have his baby, her mother was slick enough to blackmail him for a sizeable sum of money. After all, she correctly surmised that he would do anything to avoid the kind of public humiliation that caused church folks to send their leader packing. He almost chocked up sharing this last sentence with Dale.

Pastor Paisley had already told more than he intended, so he decided to "air all his dirty laundry." He had Dale's full attention. Neither man could tell you a thing about the game they were supposed to be watching. Pastor had the added dilemma of his wife wanting a divorce. He had a secret that more than one young girl was likely carrying his seed, and he "prayed" God would grant him favor by not letting all his dirty deeds become public, at least not all at once.

The solution to all his problems was money. Having revealed all of this, Pastor lowered his eyes to the floor and said, *"I need a lot of money, and fast, Dale."* He tried to see out of his peripheral vision to glean if Dale was feeling sympathetic enough to offer him as much money as he needed, without Pastor having to beg. If necessary, he was a professional beggar.

Dale now became skeptical of Pastor's motives in inviting him to his home to watch games. He knew a shady character when he met one, because he had a shady past too. Once the pastor changed his dialogue from needing money to needing Dale's money, Dale understood fully why Pastor Paisley had befriended him. Dale saw how shaken Pastor was and asked how he could help.

The Pastor told Dale he was being blackmailed by the pregnant girl's mother and didn't have the kind of money she was asking for. Dale hadn't yet shared his dilemma about cheating with women, nor had he told Pastor that his wife, too, wanted a divorce. He was keeping his secrets and lies to himself for the moment. He didn't get all his wealth from his wife's family fortune, or from his skilled ability as a lawyer. No, Dale Clyburn had a secret he did not elect to share at this moment.

Dale thought this might be the time to use Pastor Paisley, since he was so desperate for immediate funds. Dale told him he would give him whatever amount of money he needed to silence the pregnant teen's mother and to pay for a divorce and alimony. Just as Pastor breathed a deep, loud sigh of relief, Dale said he didn't intend to just *give* Paisley the money.

Dale said, *"You've heard of 'quid pro quo,' right?"* Now it was Dale's turn to use his periphery to see if Pastor understood where Dale was going with his question. Pastor knew the Latin term *"this for that,"* but stood up because he was too nervous to remain seated. What do I have to do to get this money, Dale?

Dale Clyburn had a few years earlier defended a serious drug runner, and he was skillful enough to get the defendant off with a light sentence and only a quarter million dollar fine. Dale knew he was guilty, but told himself that the best lawyers don't judge their clients. They represent them to the best of their ability.

That drug dealer was heavily into the growing, selling and distributing of every major street drug that was popular among white-collar intellectuals like Dale Clyburn. Dale was smart enough to never use drugs, but he was bold enough to accept his former client's offer to get in on the millions to be made through the drug connection between Jamaica and the United States. It was all about supply and demand, and the demand always exceeded the supply. So the price to purchase these top quality Jamaican drugs was consistently high.

Hell, lawyers, doctors, movie stars and filthy rich people didn't care how much they paid for the drugs that would help them forget their problems. Dale was greedy and seedy, so this scheme was perfect for him. He had no conscience either, so he never bothered to follow the drugs to learn how many deaths by suicide or murder they caused. He loved money, and that was his drug of choice.

Dale asked the pastor to sit because he had something important to share. Pastor Paisley would have to fly to Jamaica at least twice a month for three months, and bring back some Jamaican *"coffee."* Pastor knew it wasn't coffee he would be bringing back, but told Dale he would do it if he could be assured that he wouldn't get caught.

The pastor wanted to know how much he would get paid for each trip, and whether there would be any upfront money. Dale told him he could give him $25,000 each trip, with $15,000 upfront. Pastor's eyes made wild movements, as he processed what was happening.

Pastor Paisley was too desperate for money to think about any repercussions. This kind of cash would certainly keep him out of trouble with the girl and her mother, with some left over for his soon to be ex-wife. Dale told him the contact in Jamaica would have everything packed up and ready to pick up. If anything went wrong, Dale had an attorney in Jamaica for the pastor to call, and he would handle things. The greedy pastor and his corrupt friend, Dale had become *"strange bed fellows,"* as William Shakespeare had written a couple of centuries earlier.

The two men shook hands to signify they had a deal, and Pastor wanted to know when the first trip would be. Dale told him all his expenses would be covered, and the only thing Pastor had to do was pack his bags because the first trip was tomorrow! So, Pastor Paisley had to find someone to give his Sunday sermon, and he needed to make up a convenient lie to tell his wife.

He also needed to find a way to get word to the mother and daughter that he would have their money very soon. That should shut them up. He was told he would be gone two or three days and would stay at a five-star hotel. Pastor couldn't wait to leave! Maybe his drug of choice was money, just like Dale!

When Pastor Paisley got to the office the next day, he told Harriett Smith, the office manager, he would be going to a church revival for a few days each month for the next three months, and he wanted her to take care of everything important while he was gone. He made a few phone calls to some ministers he knew to see who could fill in for him while he was gone, and one stepped up to cover because the offering would be all his.

Harriett told him she had someone coming in for an interview to fill the assistant office manager's position, since the other one had quit and Harriett was doing the work of two people.

Harriett Smith was your typical office manager. She was average height and weight, wore thick glasses, had dull brown hair, and spoke with a slight lisp because she wore braces. Had she been wearing them since she was a teen, or were her teeth in such seriously bad shape that she needed braces for years and years? In any case, Harriett was not attractive, but she was smart and intuitive, and a "cracker-jack" office manager who more than once covered for Pastor Paisley failing to pay a bill for the church.

Harriett had begun to be suspicious about the number of members leaving the church, followed by the assistant quitting without saying anything to anyone. Pastor Paisley didn't seem alarmed at any of this, which made Harriett become just a little suspicious of him. She respected him greatly, so she pushed any thoughts that he may be a liar and a cheat out of her head.

Still, she felt a strange feeling in the pit of her stomach when Pastor told her he would be attending church revivals elsewhere and missing his own church services. Pastor had not intended to replace the Administrative Assistant who left because he had no money to pay for the position. Suddenly, he told Harriett to hire someone because things were looking good for him to expand the church. She said to herself, *"How are we gonna expand when we're bleeding from losing faithful parishioners? And HE plans to do revivals at other churches and starve his own church. How's that possible?"*

Pastor noticed Harriett was lost in thought, so he called her back to attention by adding that more money would be coming in because of a new partnership he had formed. Of course he never revealed that the name of his new partner was the rising legal star, Dale Clyburn, who was just nominated to be Lead Prosecutor for the State of Pennsylvania. He would have to go through a series of interviews, but he would get the position if he passed all the tests. All indications were that Dale Clyburn was the favorite for that promotion.

Pastor was in his office, busily taking care of last-minute details before his first trip to Jamaica, when a young lady named Chanel Bettancourt walked in with thick eyeglasses and a sort of frumpy looking appearance. Pastor Paisley assumed she was the woman for the interview for Administrative Assistant, but before he directed her to Harriett, he couldn't help but muse about the fact that the two women could have a contest for whose glasses were the thickest or whose attire was the least attractive.

She said she had an interview with a woman named Harriett, and Pastor got up and escorted her to Harriett's office. Unless Harriett was presenting Chanel as the employee choice for that particular month, Pastor didn't want to be bothered. He pulled out his calculator and started adding up the money he was about to make from these trips to Jamaica, thinking he had struck pure gold knowing Attorney Dale Clyburn.

Dale called and told him someone would be calling, and to trust the caller. This would be a piece of cake, and the money was good with a bonus thrown in for some extra stuff. The Pastor liked the sound of a bonus being thrown in, but what was the extra stuff? He dare not ask, or he might not go through with the trip.

Dale gave him the attorney's contact information in the event he had any problems while being in Jamaica, like having a missing passport or something. Pastor thought about all that was said and thought for a second, and then his heartbeat became faster as he repeated, *"Missing passport?"* He decided to focus on the fact that the money was too good to pass up and this would shut up the girl and her mother, and even his wife.

Hey, if things went well for him financially, he just might not leave Jamaica! This sleazy man of the cloth actually entertained the idea of leaving the congregation without a leader, and never bringing financial satisfaction to the pregnant teen or his wife!

The next day Pastor Elvis Paisley was ready to head to Jamaica to pick up what Dale called Jamaican coffee, and get the $25,000 to the pregnant girl and her mother. He would have more than enough to negotiate with his wife to either stay, or get a quiet divorce and not badmouth him in his church.

As promised, Dale made sure Pastor got his $15,000 upfront, and Pastor tucked $14,000 in his desk drawer for safe keeping. The Pastor mentioned that fact to Dale, adding that when he returned from Jamaica, he'd have the full $25,000 for that damn woman who was blackmailing him.

Although he would be staying and eating in luxury, he took $1,000 to Jamaica, just in case he saw something or someone he had to have! He was also thinking if things went smoothly, he would continue this gig and give up the church altogether. Who needed all those members bugging him for salvation, or prayer, or visiting some sick person in the hospital? Pastor Paisley already considered himself above all this, and he hadn't even made his first trip to Jamaica. Maybe he would start another church in Jamaica. Now that was a funny thought!

The Pastor was boarding his flight when he recognized the flight attendant, Mercedes Johannson, who was helping a passenger put a duffle bag in the overhead bin. Pastor knew her through Harriett, since she attended his church off and on with her when Mercedes wasn't working.

He quickly realized that if he recognized her, then she would recognize him when their eyes met. He would have to tell her the same bullshit lie about a revival, since he was sure she would tell Harriett she saw him on the flight. In a way, it was good because he sensed Harriett didn't believe his story about the revival. Now she would know he really *was* going to Jamaica to do God's business.

Mercedes did recognize Pastor Paisley, and approached him with a big smile. She told Pastor it was good seeing him again, and asked if he were traveling for business or pleasure. Of course, he told her about the revival, and she surprised him by asking where it would take place. She would be spending the night in Jamaica and might like to attend.

She told herself God might work on her lifelong sin of jealousy that sometimes led to rage. It certainly cost her any future with the handsome tech savvy musician, Keo Staffort after the last Happy Hour at 1400 South. Pastor was quick-witted and told her it was in Ocho Rios, knowing it was an hour from Montego Bay. Predictably, Mercedes told him she doubted she would make it since she stayed in MoBay, which was fairly close to the airport.

When Pastor Paisley landed in Jamaica, the guy who met him at the airport was a man of few words and no personality. This made Pastor question what he had gotten himself

question. The fact that he had just one option to recover his respectable and soon-to-be prosperous life gave him the courage to steady his nerves.

Despite not having his morning coffee, Pastor's hands were shaking as he gathered up the things he needed to carry with him. He ordered his hands to stop shaking, put on his jewelry, grabbed his folder and headed for the elevator. Yes, he *could* do this.

Pastor Paisley was driven to a place called *Moon Palace*. The driver got out of the car with Pastor and escorted him to one of the grand suites where Dale's contact was waiting for the Pastor. Pastor Paisley was surprised to see a white guy with dirty blonde dreadlocks, nose ring and tattoos galore on both arms. The suite had an ocean view and was beautiful and spacious.

They got down to business with the contact telling Pastor Elvis Paisley everything was ready to go, and he handed him what looked like a duffle bag that he could carry on the plane. He also told Pastor if anything went wrong to call the person Dale had told him to call. The Pastor never got to see what was in the two packages being stuffed into the duffle, but they were packaged like coffee and that was all he could smell. The label said *"Blue Mountain Coffee"* and that was good enough for him. The contact told Pastor Paisley he had reserved a block of rooms, and Pastor could go to his room and relax or enjoy the sights of Jamaica until he left town.

He handed Pastor his airline ticket for his flight out the next morning and a key to his room. Pastor felt like he could use a stiff drink, and he noticed that the hotel in which he was staying had a "Happy Hour" that was similar to the one held monthly at 1400 South. He decided he would stop by the hotel Happy Hour before going to his room.

As he ordered a glass of wine at the bar, a young woman came over and started conversing with him. He felt like he was in a country where no one knew him so he didn't mention he was a pastor. She was very flirty, but he decided he better go back to his room and stay out of trouble, fearing she could be a set up.

The next day he got to the airport and went through security without any problems even though the dogs were sniffing other passengers' bags and Pastor was trying hard not to show how nervous he was. He boarded the plane and slept on the flight, not wanting to talk to anyone because he was a little paranoid after meeting the flirty woman and being in the company of serious drug dealers. He trusted no one.

Once safely in his own home, he couldn't wait to call Dale to tell him everything went smoothly and he was glad to be back home. Dale told him he would have someone from his office pick up the package and bring him a little extra bonus for his uneventful first trip.

Pastor Elvis Paisley had his promised money, and then some! He had no drugs in his possession any more, so he figured he was free to resume his normal business. As he drove home, he realized he had told Harriett Smith that he was going on a revival. She was sharp, so he knew he better offer a convincing story about where he had been the past two days. He would worry about that when he returned to work the following Monday. His first concern was making sure his congregation believed his lies that Sunday. He'd deal with Harriett on Monday.

Pastor also needed a credible story to tell the congregants about being away at a church revival. He conjured up a story that the series of revivals would be in Jamaica, and there would be Christians from around the world attending religious services held to inspire and gain new converts. He would tell them that these spiritual revivals started in the evening and went until daybreak without anyone noticing the passing of time.

Pastor Elvis Paisley spoke to his congregation that Sunday, and he made passionate statements designed to stir up his audience. *"My friends, I tell you that Christian people gathered together who were suddenly aware of God's presence, HIS power guiding, directing, and leading them. The essence of the revival was a visitation of by Holy Spirit coming down upon the people and upon the church.*

I partnered with a group of ministers who do this every month, and I'm sure you'll be proud of your Pastor because I receive a hefty stipend for my services that will benefit the church. Now isn't that just like our God to prosper us by sending me to Jamaica a few times in as many months? My ministry is where God sends me! Amen? Amen!" Of course, he seized that moment to say that God told him to tell his congregation to give according to what each member was hearing in the Holy Spirit.

He was so convincing that he paused in his money pitch and asked the congregation to be especially quiet so they could hear God and feel His presence. As they were listening to the true and living God, they were reaching for wallets and checkbooks as if in a trance. Some congregants probably didn't know how much they gave that Sunday, until they woke that Monday and didn't have enough to pay their bills.

Pastor took in the biggest single collection of his career in ministry, and only he and God knew that everything he uttered from the pulpit that Sunday was a lie. Had he no fear of God's wrath against disobedient sinners? Pastor Elvis Paisley was among the biggest sinners in God's eyes because he dared to wear the pastor's collar and let people think he had a direct pipeline to God Almighty. He couldn't help but think to himself, *"Wow, first I get a huge sum of money just for being a traveler to Jamaica, and then I get my flock to give extra generously because their leader brought revival to the unsaved in Jamaica! Life doesn't get any better than this!"*

Pastor Elvis Paisley couldn't wait until church was over and the people were gone, so he could count up all the cash in the envelope he had received from the person

Dale sent to pick up the "coffee." Plus, he knew he had $14,000 in his desk drawer. He would pay off the girl and her mother, and also give his soon-to-be ex-wife some cash, telling her the same story as the congregants about the church revival and how he will soon be attending several others. It was past dinnertime by the time he got his money counted, and he knew he had more than enough to rid himself of his immediate personal problems.

When Pastor Paisley unlocked his office door, everything seemed in order. The space was tidy, just like he left it. Still, he felt the need to rush to his desk drawer to get the $14,000 that he alone knew was there. He locked his office, but never his desk.

The envelope with the money was gone! He called Harriett to see if anything went on while he was gone, and she told him everything was fine. He asked her if the Pastor who filled in for him had been in his office, and she told him yes, but she checked the office when he was done and everything was in its place. Harriett didn't see what Pastor was so emotional about, but she kept those words to herself.

Pastor Paisley was burning mad, but didn't want to reveal to Harriett that he had that kind of money in a desk drawer. He trusted Harriett and believed her when she told him everything was fine.

Harriett said to herself that it probably wasn't the right time to ask how the revival went, but she was excited to hear all about it that Monday morning. She was not a member of his congregation, so she missed his sharing the details of the revival. He would have to muster up the same level of excitement, and tell his story all over again to Harriett.

Pastor went through his desk searching for anything with the young girl's name or anything that might incriminate him. Then he realized the envelope had the note in it.

Now, he was thinking the girl and her mother might be the thieves, since he missed the deadline to pay Mom by a day. Could they have been bold enough to ask Harriett if they could leave a "church business" note on Pastor's desk? If so, Harriett would have taken their note, but not let them in the office. No, the blackmailer didn't take the money.

Pastor Paisley also speculated that there could have been a professional break in by some of Dale's drug smuggling people who could get away with stealing some money from Pastor because Pastor would be helpless to do anything about it. These types of people could break into an office and leave, without disturbing the dust in the air. So having his trusted, but despicable new friend Dale take back some of Pastor's "hard earned" money could be an explanation for the theft.

Pastor Paisley needed that $14,000 badly, but, thankfully, with the money from his first trip to Jamaica and the unexpected bonus, he felt he could still silence the teen, the mother and the wife. He would never be so careless again by leaving a large amount of cash in an unlocked drawer in his office. Lesson definitely learned!

Chapter 8
Some Lives Get More Complicated

Office Manager, Harriett Smith hired Chanel "Shay" Bettancourt to work as her Administrative Assistant in Pastor Elvis Paisley's office. This was her first experience working in a Non-Denominational Church, but Chanel was a spiritual being who was very familiar with the power of prayer. She was set to start first thing Monday morning. Harriett's mind was now curiously on what had made Pastor so agitated. After all, she was a seasoned administrator and would never have let a visiting pastor leave the office in disarray.

"It looked the same when he left as it did when he came, and Pastor Elvis Paisley should have been grateful to me for making sure of that! What's the point of coming back from a powerful revival in a foul mood? He better straighten up before the new Administrative Assistant starts Monday. I

certainly don't want to drive her away." Harriett sat at her desk making a list of the responsibilities she was going to give Chanel Bettancourt. Yes there was a job description on file, but this was Harriett's opportunity to change it before Chanel knew anything different.

Pastor Paisley was frantic to find the missing $14,000. He wasn't just worried about the money because he had a big secret attached to it and didn't want anyone else using his indiscretion with a teen in his church against him. The thought that the thief may have been someone connected to his Jamaican trips unnerved him because he was about to make a second run in less than two weeks. He would never leave money in his desk or anywhere in his office again. That was a fact!

Pastor had to pull himself together, wipe the sweat from his forehead, upper lip and hands, and then go home to his wife. When he got home, he kissed her on the cheek, knowing he didn't deserve the lips. Still, she pulled away and wiped her sleeve across her whole cheek and mouth. She was still hurt from his public betrayal of her trust. She wouldn't turn her own husband in to the police for statutory rape, but she wanted to hit him hard in the most vulnerable spot on his body.

Pastor's wife had been too humiliated to attend church that Sunday, so she missed his elaborate speech to the congregation about the amazing revival he had attended. She also missed hearing that he was now part of a group of pastors determined to bring salvation to poor people in Jamaica. They would be traveling back and forth on a regular basis.

Pastor cleared his throat and drank a glass of water before speaking to his wife. He needed the courage to present his bold lie to the woman who knew him best, and he felt deep down that she could discern whether or not he was giving her a line of bullshit. Of course he was! The church folks accepted it, and even gave more generously than usual. Maybe he could use that piece of information to strengthen his story.

Pastor Paisley told his wife he had great news, and began to share the church lie, speaking with the conviction of a newly saved sinner. He never made eye contact with her, but deliberately used voice inflection to stress certain points. Oh, he was going to make a difference in the lives of those without a voice, and he was going to be paid a handsome sum of money for having a generous heart.

At first, Pastor's wife wasn't impressed. But then he said he had the whole $25,000 that the teen congregant's mother was demanding. Now he had his wife's full attention. She sat down and looked directly at him, which made him both nervous and happy. He continued to say he would reach out to the greedy mother to arrange to give her the money. His wife insisted she be present when delivered the money, and he took that to mean she wanted to be his witness if that mother ever dared to claim she was never paid.

In truth, his wife wanted to observe the passing of the money from her unfaithful husband to the corrupt member of the congregation, after which she was leaving him. Her bags were already packed and hidden in the hall closet.

She would transfer them discreetly into her car sometime early on the morning they would be bringing the hush money to the pregnant teen's mother. As soon as the transaction was over, she would get into her car, drive off, and never speak to Pastor Elvis Paisley again, except through her attorney.

She had suffered her last and most embarrassing humiliation by being the wife of this "man of God!"

Pastor Paisley called the girl, who answered the phone. Her mother quickly snatched the phone from her and said, *"I recognize your voice, my lying leader, and all I want to know is where is my money?"* Pastor said sarcastically that he had her damn money and wanted to know only when and where he could meet her. *"Did you just curse at me, Pastor?"* He replied, *"All I said was I have your darn money. It was the Devil that made you hear otherwise."*

They met an hour later at a gas station, and while Pastor and this mother pretended to get gas, he slipped an envelope of cash into the oversize purse the woman was carrying. She immediately pressed her whole arm over the opening in her purse, got in her car and drove off without saying a word to Pastor Paisley or his wife, who stood at his side. The teen wasn't present.

Once the woman was out of sight, Pastor's wife got into their car without a word. She had a disgusted look on her face. As soon as they pulled into the driveway of their home, she got out of the car, tossed him her house keys, and jumped into her car parked on the other side of the driveway.

He stared in disbelief, thinking this must be some kind of a joke. But then he noticed the back seat was full with her suitcases and some personal items. She was leaving for real, and he couldn't do anything to stop her or cause her to want to come inside with him. She was going out of his life forever, and he was left to tell the congregation whatever lie sounded best to him.

Pastor Elvis Paisley spent a restless night. He almost cried thinking about the missing money and who could have taken it. He feared falling apart and getting arrested at the airport on the next trip to Jamaica. He worried about growing his congregation again. He grieved over the loss of his wife because he did love her very much. But he deserved to lose her. He wanted to feel proud of getting the money for the pregnant teen, but he was ashamed instead. He used to be an honorable man and now he was the most repugnant man of God he had ever met.

Monday morning arrived, and Pastor arrived at his office by 8:00 a.m., as usual. Both Harriett and Chanel were already there. As soon as Chanel was formally introduced to

Pastor, she was immediately smitten with his charm. All her life she wanted to meet a real "man of the cloth," one who wasn't afraid to dedicate himself to the Lord.

Had she found her "Boaz," and if so, would God reveal to Pastor that Chanel was the woman he wanted and needed to marry? After all, in the Book of Ruth in the *Holy Bible*, God made sure Boaz noticed Ruth, and then he fell in love with her and they married. Chanel was Ruth!

Chanel was so lost in romantic thoughts that she didn't hear him welcome her until he grabbed her hand and shook it firmly. He told her to simply call him "Pastor." *"Call me 'Shay.' Everyone who knows me calls me that."* She looked a bit frumpy, wearing, loose, big clothing, so no one knew what size she was.

She had poor posture, so at first glance you would think she looked like someone's elderly grandmother. But when you looked at her face, you realized she wasn't thirty years old, and you wished she were open to the suggestion of a complete makeover.

Shay was not shy, but had a subdued way about her because she didn't look at anyone when she interacted with people. She wore thick eyeglasses that looked like *Coke* bottles because she had high minus lenses for nearsightedness. Shay had a beautiful face and had been told she looked like the actress, Halle Berry when not wearing her eyeglasses. She was hoping to have laser eye surgery done sometime in the near future so she wouldn't have to wear glasses or contact lenses.

Shay was bi-racial, with a European-American father and an African-American mother. She didn't have friends because it was hard for her to socialize with people who weren't sure of her heritage, and she never felt attractive. Shay had received a substantial inheritance from her late grandmother, and that allowed her to live at 1400 South with her pet parrot, Sugar, who only knew how to say, *"Thank you, Jesus,"* and *"How you doin'?"*

Chanel Bettancourt had grown up in the church, with her father being the minister and her mother playing the organ every Sunday. She also knew what happened behind the scenes of a church with everyone wanting to meet with her father to discuss their problems. She surmised that the members of this congregation had the same attraction to their spiritual leader as the congregation of her youth had for her father.

Chanel remembered how many women had found her father attractive, and how they even made up problems just to be in his presence. She remembered finding their behavior detestable, and here she was feeling like she was butter in the hands of Pastor Elvis Paisley. She felt guilty at first and tried not to let on that he made her heart beat fast whenever they interacted.

By her third day on the job, Pastor told her she was doing a great job, and she started bringing him coffee and breakfast sandwiches from *Dunkin' Donuts* when she got to work each morning after that. He thanked her each time, but finally said, *"Listen, Chanel, I mean 'Shay,' take money from the petty cashbox to buy me breakfast, but don't keep spending your own money."*

When Shay went into the petty cash box, she was surprised to find that there was at least $1,000, all in $100 bills. She took one bill, thinking she would buy a week of breakfast sandwiches before she would need to return to the petty cash box. She didn't remember her father having that much money in his petty cashbox, but shrugged it off, telling herself this was a more affluent congregation.

The two of them became so comfortable with each other that Harriett felt a little jealous. She was the seasoned Office Manager and Chanel was the brand new Administrative Assistant. Harriett thought she noticed them talking in whispers and stopping when she entered the room. Could she be paranoid? Of course not!

Shay was working on notes for Pastor's next *Bible Study*, when Pastor came to her desk and told her he had something he wanted to discuss with her. He told Shay his wife had just left him and was going to divorce him over something he did that he regretted. He told her he wanted to tell her and Harriett before anyone else, and he had already shared the grim news with Harriett.

Shay was shocked and happy at the same time, so she acted sympathetic, telling him God would forgive him for whatever sins he committed against his wife. All she could do was think about what he must be going through and how she could give him a sympathetic ear.

Despite being a bit prudish, Shay fantasized about the day she would give him both ears and the rest of her body. Shay started sprucing herself up since the Pastor was going to be single soon. It never occurred to her that he loved his wife and would do anything to take back his indiscretion. She set her sights on Pastor Paisley and was going to do everything in her power to win her prize. Once in a while, a man she saw twice on television would meet with the Pastor behind closed doors. Harriett told her the name was Mr. Dale Clyburn, and he was a very important man.

Shay listened intently whenever Pastor, in weak moments, shared his tender thoughts about his wife, his finances, and his impact on his congregation. As he took the weekly typed notes she had prepared for him for *Bible Study*, he always thanked her for being his sounding board. He liked that she didn't socialize with anyone in church, or gossip with the women always running to him about something petty. She intuitively knew how and when to interrupt him, saying another client was either waiting or on the phone. So Pastor was extra grateful that Chanel was astute enough to know how to get rid of pesky parishioners taking up all Pastor Paisley's time.

Harriett told Shay kiddingly that she thought Shay was smitten with the Pastor. Shay denied it, but knew that Harriett was no fool and Shay better put some distance between Pastor and herself.

Pastor announced that it was time for the second revival in Jamaica, where dozens of prominent pastors and spiritual leaders would be gathering to address the needs of the poor and unsaved. They understood it would be difficult to reach him by phone while he was gone, which meant they would handle whatever came up in his absence. He would be back before the next Sunday service, so he didn't need a substitute pastor to sit in his office or preach to his congregation.

Chanel felt comfortable in her new position because she truly understood what parishioners needed and what Pastor Paisley needed. Actually, she thought she would try to find a way to be more than an Administrative Assistant to her new boss who was going through a divorce and having trouble in the church. What a combination! Her tender heart, normally guarded, was open to Pastor Elvis Paisley, even if he had yet to discover that door.

Chanel had just gotten home from work, when a fellow resident passing by her to get to the elevator said, *"Hey, Shay, you coming to Happy Hour? You never come, but it's so much fun. You should try it sometime."* Shay had heard about Happy Hour but wasn't interested in attending, since she didn't drink and didn't think she had anything in common with those attending. In her mind she thought people who drank, smoke and cussed were Satan's children and she wanted no association with those "heathens."

As Shay got her mail and headed for the elevator to relax in her unit for the evening, she noticed people bringing in food, banquet equipment, and flowers for the evening's Happy Hour. The lobby area was bustling with folks, so she scooted past them and got on the elevator without speaking to anyone.

Shay wanted to get inside her "sanctuary," undress and slip into something comfortable, but unstylish, and read scriptures from the *Holy Bible*. Before she knew it, she was kneeling and weeping softly, asking God for forgiveness, even though nothing happened between her and Pastor. She knew the scriptures well, and recited the one that says if you break one of the Commandments, you've broken them all. Then there was the one about lusting in your heart being a sin.

Shay was definitely having sexual thoughts about Pastor Paisley, and she knew she was doing a terrible job of keeping her desire a secret from Harriett. She repeated, *"Devil, I rebuke you!"* but the more she fought Satan, the keener her instincts became for finding reasons to be close to her Pastor. She knew she had to do something to control her feelings for him, and yet, in her mind, she was certain he felt the same about her.

Why else would he confide in her about the problems in his marriage? He wanted Shay to know he would be unattached very soon. *"Yes,"* Shay told herself, *"he knows I want to feel his tender touch, and he undresses me with his eyes. Neither of us has found the right mate in life yet, but we're meant to be together now. God brought me to this job to meet my Boaz!"*

When Chanel got in bed that night, she tossed and turned, unable to fall asleep. Her mind battles were between choosing to serve Satan and God. Satan won! She was only half asleep when she had visions of Pastor Paisley fondling her and making love to her. She never resisted his advances, but instead let her body go limp as he held her so tightly that she almost fainted from lack of oxygen.

Then she caught herself, and said aloud, *"Devil, I rebuke you!"* But she knew as she was masturbating that Devil knew her rebuke was weak and insincere. She lay there, praying for rest, when she heard her parrot Sugar say, *"Devil, I rebuke you." "Devil, I rebuke you." "Devil, I rebuke you!"* That noisy parrot almost interrupted her orgasm, but she completed her fantasy dream with her index finger. As she rose to go to the bathroom to wash her face and hands, she threw a blanket over Sugar's cage. *"Go to sleep before I send you to meet the Devil! Now rebuke THAT!"*

Chanel and Harriett were starting to become friends, and Harriett had begun to share more than office procedures with her. Harriett was tired of stepping out of the office or into the bathroom to take confidential calls from confused or angry members of the congregation. She was also tired of riffling through the mail to find letters that might compromise the Pastor's integrity.

It was Shay's job to open and sort the mail, and Harriett had more than enough to do. She volunteered to Shay that the good Pastor must be involved in some un-Christian activities, based on calls and a few correspondences that had come through to the office. Shay's eyes widened and her mouth opened slightly because she didn't want to hear anything bad about Pastor Elvis Paisley. Still, she trusted Harriett's judgment, so she had a real dilemma on her mind.

Harriett passed the pile of unopened mail to Shay, who immediately sat down at her desk. All Shay could think about was being noticed by the Pastor and hoping he would want to take her out for coffee or lunch. After all, within twenty-four hours, she had gotten her hair done, nails polished, and even put on some pale lipstick. Since her hair was short, the stylist didn't have to do much with it. The woman dried Shay's hair and brushed it back with her fingers. She remarked that Shay's whole face opened up, and both women were quite surprised at how good she looked.

"Well, Miss Chanel, you look marvelous. Got a date tonight?" Chanel didn't have the heart to say she was going home to a parrot, but had gotten her hair done so her boss and Pastor would notice her in the morning. She said nothing, but smiled weakly.

Shay couldn't do much about her unattractive clothes, but the next morning, she found a brightly colored scarf in the bottom drawer of her dresser, and she tied it in a loose knot around her neck. It added some color to her appearance, and she was certain Pastor would notice. Oh, wait! She forgot he said he was leaving town for a second revival. Shay wondered if she had the time or energy to create another "new image" when he returned from Jamaica.

She decided to forget about beauty and seduction for a day, and do her job by opening and sorting the mail in a timely manner. She told herself to focus and stop being distracted. That was enough chastisement for one day. While opening one of the envelopes, she was floored by what she was reading. The letter was addressed to Pastor Elvis Paisley, calling him a low down, dirty rotten, scoundrel. Shay was appalled because she instinctively defended Pastor in her mind. But by the time she finished reading about the "charges" against the spiritual leader of the church, she sat there in disbelief and a little shock.

The person writing the letter told him she wanted her money back from an investment he asked the congregants to invest in. Apparently, Pastor had convinced several congregants that every investor would make some money and have a little financial freedom. If they each gave him $1000, then he assured them that he would give them

$3,000 back. Who could resist that offer, coming from the head of the church?

The congregant had written that she trusted and believed in him, and he was a fraud, and she was going to report him to the proper authorities. Shay refused to believe any of this. The Pastor was an honest man and would never dupe anybody! Or would he?

She couldn't wait to see him next, and in the meantime, she put the letter aside to ask Harriett if she knew anything about an investment. Shay put the letter aside, and then opened another envelope that shared the same sentiment. Both letters were unsigned.

By the time Shay finished opening all the mail, there were five letters saying the same thing, but Shay didn't want to believe it. Harriett was in her office when Shay entered, carrying all five letters. Her face must have shown some discomfort, if not outright disbelief, because Harriett said, *"Chanel, you came to work today looking better than you ever have before. You were in a great mood. Now what's wrong?"*

Shay sat heavily in the seat across from Harriett and placed the five letters on Harriett's desk, one at a time. Harriett glanced at one of them, but didn't bother to touch or read any of them. Shay looked confused at first, but then realized Harriett must have seen these types of letters recently, and these were just five more.

Harriett gathered her thoughts and then spoke directly to Shay. *"I know that Pastor has been taking money from the congregants for an investment he packaged as a 'sure thing.' But the details have yet to be revealed to them – and to me! All they know is he promised to double or triple whatever dollars they gave him."* Harriett admitted to being suspicious of his activities lately, and she also knew about his duping the congregants out of their hard-earned money. These were credible people sending letters. Harriett believed them over Pastor Paisley, but would never confront him about the situation. At least, she wouldn't do it right now.

Harriett told Chanel she knew for a fact that this wasn't the first time her boss had done this to the congregation, and she added that if Chanel weren't so blinded by her infatuation with him, she would have grasped the sad fact that people were slowly leaving the church. There used to be close to a hundred members, but now there were thirty-five "on a good Sunday."

Chanel was shocked and couldn't believe what she was hearing. Harriett told her that was yet another reason his wife was divorcing him, and although he worked and received money from his congregation every week, he wasn't using it to support his family. She was tired of him going from one "get rich quick" scheme to another, and having nothing to show for it except embarrassment and humiliation. As his wife, she suffered that, too.

Shay walked out of Harriett's office in silence. She started thinking about the church members and wondering who sent the letters. There were some really nice elderly people whom she couldn't help thinking about because they were on fixed incomes. She began to replace her infatuation for Pastor Elvis Paisley with anger and disgust for him. She decided she needed some fresh air, and told Harriett she would go home for lunch. She had some "soul searching" to do.

All the way home, Shay was distracted from driving in the safe manner all drivers are supposed to exhibit. She heard a horn honk loudly behind her because the light had turned green and she hadn't moved into the intersection. She was startled by the horn, and jerked her car forward when she did move.

She knew she better focus on the road or she might not make it home.

Shay greeted her parrot and then made a curried chicken salad with leftover chicken breast she had in the refrigerator. She put it on a bed of salad greens and had some flavored sparkling water. Since she had been so disciplined about eating a healthy meal, she treated herself to some *Patti LaBelle Apple Cobbler* for dessert.

After eating, she didn't want to go back to work but she knew she had to. While driving back, Shay told herself she was a fool to have been so blinded by her boss' attention. Was she really that love-starved? When she got back in the office, Harriett told her that the day's mail had come, and in it were three more letters to the Pastor saying the same thing about him duping the congregation.

Chanel had previously glanced through some of the files in order to familiarize herself with the members who tithed, and those who gave offerings. Now she felt compelled to go through all the files, even the ones kept separately in Pastor's office. There were more files stored in an empty office. Harriett saw files all over the place and asked Chanel what was going on. Chanel was honest with her, stating that while on lunch break, she had reached out to an attorney and was going to bring down Pastor Elvis Paisley because he was a scoundrel to defraud those innocent parishioners. Many were elderly, and still he had the audacity to rob them! *"Wow, Chanel, that was quite a lunch break you had, to go from loving to hating your boss."*

Harriett shared what the Pastor had done with a young girl in the congregation, saying that the last straw for his wife came when the mother of the girl came and told him what he had done with an underage child. She was going to press charges and have him locked up for a very long time. Harriett had actually told Pastor behind closed doors that she was thinking of turning him in, and the only way she wouldn't do that is if he changed his ways. He needed to make restitution to every single member of the congregation from whom he took money.

Naturally, Pastor Paisley promised to do everything Harriett asked, but as soon as he was out of her sight, he did nothing. Finally, Harriett couldn't take any more of his bullshit and wanted out. Shay told Harriett, *"I can't believe what a monster he is, and to think I was falling in love with him!"* Harriett told her,

"I saw how you looked at him the first day you met him. I knew he was trouble, but couldn't tell you since you were so smitten with him."

Harriett knew Shay was over being smitten by the crooked man of God, and she felt that finally, she had an ally. She no longer felt helpless to make a change, and thought she might actually do something to bring this corrupt man down. She hugged Shay and told her they would get him, and she wondered if he was bold enough to stay in Jamaica, where no one knew his name until he revealed it. If he had any idea what these two honest women were about to do to shake the core of his corrupt world, he would surely stay in Jamaica. But he didn't!

Chanel now had complete faith and trust in Harriett, and she had complete disdain for Pastor Paisley. Shay remembered that Attorney Armani Johnson lived in her building, and she felt comfortable calling her to reveal what has been going on in church, right under the noses of parishioners. Shay knew Armani specialized in divorces, but she felt that Armani would take this case since it involved gross injustice.

Chanel had access to an online copy of the directory for all residents at 1400 South, and it was easy to get the number she needed. She and Harriett went into Harriett's office and closed the door, even though they were alone in the office. Attorney Armani Johnson's assistant answered the phone, and tactfully asked what the problem was, rather than to honor Shay's request to be put directly through to the attorney. She put Chanel on hold, and returned to the phone a full two minutes later.

The assistant said Ms. Johnson was very busy, but would review any material they wished to send to her attention. Harriett and Chanel promised to bring a thick file to Armani's office the next day. The assistant promised to alert Armani that these women were coming.

Meanwhile, Armani was sitting in her plush office, deep in thought about what to do about Katherine Clyburn. She knew it would be a conflict of interest for her to take Katherine's divorce case against Dale Clyburn, since he was Armani's mystery man, *"Mr. Prosecutor"* about whom a few office staff and friends had spoken. No one knew his name, and Katherine had no clue yet about her husband's extra-marital relationship with Armani.

What a twist of events for Katherine to reach out to Armani to represent her! Armani only half listened when her assistant told her that Chanel Bettancourt and Harriett Smith would be coming the next day to bring a large file of information against Pastor Elvis Paisley. She quickly agreed to meet the ladies, dismissing her assistant so she could think some more about Katherine.

Armani was astute and proactive, so when she suspected Dale was cheating on both her and his wife, she hired a private investigator to follow Dale and report his findings to Armani. This shrewd, and very expensive investigator dug deep into Dale's background over the last few years, even reviewing his high profile work cases to see if anything inappropriate were going on with some of the people he defended.

The private investigator was scheduled to share his findings with Armani in two days, and her newest dilemma was whether or not to share with Katherine Clyburn what she would learn about the unscrupulous Dale Clyburn, Esquire. Armani had stopped wrestling with herself about representing Katherine and risking disbarment, but she felt a need to tell Katherine what she knew, just "woman-to-woman." After that, Armani would be sure to recommend a top-notch divorce attorney, promising Katherine she would surely win her case.

Armani briefly turned her attention to her calendar, where her assistant had noted that Harriett Smith and Chanel Bettancourt would see her tomorrow with incriminating documents against their crooked spiritual leader. She specialized in divorces, but was intrigued at the idea of taking down a "jackleg preacher" who stole from his church members.

Unfortunately, the timing was off. Her mission right now was to see Dale Clyburn begging for forgiveness from her and Katherine because he was eventually going to know who was the mastermind behind his fall. She again entertained the possibility of representing Katherine, thinking the two of them would be a formidable force against the high and mighty rising star, Attorney Dale Clyburn. Armani had to remind herself out loud that to represent Katherine Clyburn would be unethical and she could be disbarred if her colleagues found out.

Armani instructed her assistant to clear her calendar and hold all calls for the time the investigator would be meeting to present his secret findings about Dale Clyburn. She needed complete privacy with the "client" who would be meeting with her behind closed doors.

When the investigator arrived, he placed a really thick file on Armani's desk, pulled out of it a notebook containing a summary of his findings. He started by saying Armani was correct to suspect Dale Clyburn of dirty dealings, but that she had no idea how deep in crime Dale actually was.

"First of all, Dale Clyburn accepted a few low-level bribes from clients asking him to ignore certain privileged information when representing them. So Dale complied, winning cases he should have lost because his clients really had indefensible arguments." Armani listened intently to the private investigator, as he pulled from the large folder a couple of small files detailing the cases about which he was speaking.

"I interviewed a judge who said he knew Dale had "twisted the evidence" to make the innocent plaintiff look guilty, but sometimes the law works against you because the judge couldn't prove Dale had done anything wrong. The judge noted that Dale could not look the person in the face when the trial was over."

Armani interrupted the private investigator. "No doubt he knew he had done something totally against the principles he held dear when he first became a lawyer. That man was the one I was attracted to, but then he changed right before my eyes. I watched him get greedy and lose all those principles in less than a year."

The private investigator then pulled from the big folder a large file containing all the legal documents pertaining to the high profile case Dale had won when he defended a member of a notable underworld crime family. When Dale won that case, it put him in line to be considered for the position of Lead Prosecutor for the State of Pennsylvania.

"Looks like your man Dale Clyburn will get that big job in a couple of weeks, but wait until you hear what happened after he won the case that launched his career into the 'big leagues.' Take a look at this!" The private investigator passed some depositions for Armani to peruse, and at first glance, she could tell these were witnesses at the big trial, whose testimonies were never presented in the courtroom.

Someone paid someone off to bury these statements because they correctly incriminated the defendant. Dale was as much interested in winning to make himself look good as he was to earn the hefty fee his client was paying him.

Armani reached for a legal pad to take some notes, even though everything the private investigator was saying was supported by the documents in her hand and in the fat folder. Still, she was nervously excited at how potentially easy it would be to take down the powerful rising star, Dale Clyburn.

Too bad the glory would go to whoever Armani recommended to defend Katherine Clyburn. If only Armani Johnson could be the attorney of record, then she would surely be the one whose name was presented to be the next Lead Prosecutor for the State of Pennsylvania! Dale would be promoted to a small jail cell!

Armani had to pull herself back to the conversation at hand. She heard the private investigator's next words in the middle of his sentence, so she cleared her throat and reached for the water sitting next to her desktop. As she drank, dramatically touching her throat as the water went down, she asked the investigator to say his last sentence again.

"Dale got this high level crime boss off with a light sentence and a heavy fine, which caused the guy's brother to approach Dale on another matter. He proposed that Dale could make a fortune coordinating drug runs between the United States and Jamaica. His risk would be low because the criminals hiring him had purchased the "services" of customs agents, judges, lawyers and law enforcement in Jamaica, and they already had several United States judges and cops in their pockets.

Even if some low ranking honest cop arrested Dale anywhere along his journey between the two countries, Dale would be released within the hour. The kind of money they were talking about was $90,000 to $100,000 cash in Dale's hands after each trip. The ruse would be that Dale was coordinating shipments of expensive coffee from Jamaica to the USA."

Armani had to stop the investigator to get clarity on what she was hearing. "Are you saying that Dale involved himself in illegal drug trafficking, after doing illegal things to get an illegal criminal a lighter sentence than he deserved?" The private investigator nodded affirmatively. He said this had been going on for several months, with no sign of it stopping.

The investigator then explained that he followed Dale to Jamaica on two occasions, each time making sure to stay at the same hotel so he could monitor Dale's actions. He took plenty of incriminating photos of Dale with known drug dealers, who passed duffel bags to Dale. The outside of the bags were labeled with some exotic "coffee" name, but the private investigator got lucky one time when the dealer opened the bag to show Dale several neatly stacked piles of $100 bills. The investigator's camera just clicked away, capturing the whole thing for Armani's use later. Armani looked hard at the photos of Dale holding a duffel bag full of money that didn't belong to him.

The investigator said that the previous week, he caught an early flight and arrived at the hotel ahead of Dale. He didn't need more evidence, but wanted to see if maybe Dale was involved in other seedy activities.

Well, Dale never showed up, according to the private investigator. Instead it was some guy wearing a pastor's collar and a modest suit, looking totally out of place. The investigator didn't know this man, but since he checked into the room Dale usually occupied, he became a "person of interest."

Sure enough, the investigator followed this pastor, who picked up duffel bags of the same expensive "coffee" Dale carried, and the pastor was preparing to bring it back to the United States. *"It's funny how large sums of cash produce an entirely different aroma from the smell of fresh coffee. Greedy people always get caught in the end."* Armani shook her head in agreement.

"This pastor's name is – let me see, it's in my notes here. Yes, 'Elvis Paisley.' The second time I saw this pastor, he wasn't wearing a minister's collar, but had a brightly colored shirt coming out of that modest suit.

I followed him, not knowing if he would be meeting Dale or someone else. He was sitting at the bar at the Happy Hour in his hotel, drinking a glass of wine. A local prostitute approached him with a tease in her voice and deep cleavage in her breasts. He was most definitely interested in this woman, but he looked around the room suspiciously and then left her standing at the bar.

There's a few photos about his activities in a folder I marked 'Paisley,' even though the name won't mean anything to you. This pastor is as crooked as the lawyer, and they are some kind of tag-team, exchanging drugs for money."

The private investigator finished his verbal report, knowing it would take Armani a few days to digest all the information she had received. She reached into her desk drawer for her private checkbook, and wrote a check for the investigator's fee, adding a $100 tip. He thanked her, asked her to call him if she needed any follow up or other tasks done.

As he was leaving, the private investigator snapped his finger as if to remind him of something. *"One more thing. I almost forgot to mention that when I did some digging into this Paisley's past, I found that the reason he needed so much money was that he couldn't keep it in his pants and got some underage girl in his congregation pregnant. There's lots of talk about that going on. Might explain how he got caught up in the Clyburn mess in Jamaica. No charge for that extra information!"* His normally serious face revealed a sight smile as he left.

Armani closed the door behind him, insisting that her assistant continue to hold her calls until further notice. She knew there was an open-and-shut case against Dale, but wasn't sure which of her attorney friends deserved this high profile win. She'd name the person later, but right now, she wanted to review all the material, read all the depositions and look over all the photos.

When she finished, she hadn't realized that her assistant and everyone else in her office building had left for the evening. Only a custodian was milling about, cleaning the offices. She was hungry and exhausted, but couldn't decide if it were more important to eat or sleep. She felt certain she couldn't do both.

She decided to go home, taking the confidential files home with her. No one must know what she knows until she is ready to reveal it in a court of law. On the way home, Armani remembered that when reviewing the files, she had noticed a picture of Dale talking to a flight attendant before boarding the plane to come home from Jamaica a week ago.

She recognized the woman as Mercedes Johannson, who lived at 1400 South with Armani. They knew each other. She speculated that Dale was probably getting Mercedes' number so he could meet up with her when they were back in the States. What a rotten man he was to use his professional status and charm to woo another unsuspecting female into his web of lust and corruption!

The next morning, Armani was at work bright and early. She checked her appointments, asking her assistant to add Katherine Clyburn to her schedule that day. She planned to share everything with Katherine, promising to introduce her to the attorney who could best represent her interests. Dale had no idea he was about to lose everything. He went about his business just as confident and egotistical as ever. Armani actually delighted at the prospect of Dale in jail.

Her assistant reminded her that the two ladies from the church were her first appointment. Armani wanted to fully focus on the case against Dale, now that she had overwhelming evidence from the private investigator she hired.

She thought of this meeting with clergy folks as an annoying interruption, but she didn't get her stellar reputation by insulting clients. So she told her assistant to buzz her about an important meeting she needed to attend, if the conference with Chanel Bettancourt and Harriett Smith didn't end within half an hour of their arrival.

Meanwhile, Chanel and Harriett were preparing for their meeting with Attorney Armani Johnson. Chanel had to gather her files, along with the cashbox containing $800 in petty cash, plus the envelope full of $14,000 cash to bring to Armani's office. With Harriett's help, Chanel had a large file full of evidence against the crooked pastor, but she made sure to put the latest five letters of complaint on top of the pile of papers.

Then she started thinking back to the people who had come to the office for "special" meetings with Pastor. One face stood out because Chanel had seen him on television receiving praise for winning a high-profile case. Chanel looked through Pastor's appointment book to find the name of "Dale Clyburn." He was the man she remembered. She wondered what someone like him would be doing at Pastor's church. It didn't look like they ever prayed together, but she made a note to tell the attorney about that, too.

Chanel was unaware that Dale had come pretty regularly to Pastor's church, or that he and Pastor spent time watching sports together. Even with Dale's sizeable offering in the plate each Sunday that he attended church Pastor should never have had $14,000 in cash in his desk drawer.

What neither Chanel nor Harriett knew was that Dale had called one of the congregants while Pastor was on his first trip to Jamaica. Pastor should never have told Dale he was leaving $14,000 in his desk drawer, but on the other hand, they were supposed to be partners, so Pastor would have no reason not to trust Dale.

This particular church member was the one who cleaned Pastor's office weekly, and Dale remembered his name because Pastor said it once when Dale had come to watch sports with Pastor. So he found the man's number, called and asked him to do Dale a special favor.

The congregant was happy to be called by someone like Dale, who Pastor Paisley spoke highly of on two occasions when his parishioner cleaned up his office each week.

The favor Dale requested was for the congregant to pick up an envelope in the Pastor's desk and bring it to Dale when he was done cleaning the place. Dale told him he had spoken with Pastor earlier about picking up the envelope Pastor had left for Dale. However, since Dale was tied up in meetings, he would show his gratitude to the custodian by compensating him well for his troubles. It seemed like such a simple, credible plan.

The congregant finished cleaning the church, and then went over to Pastor's desk and opened it. Sure enough, he saw the thick envelope full of more cash than he had seen in his whole life!

The man knew it was the envelope Dale was expecting, and he hid the envelope among his cleaning supplies before leaving the office. However, once he got into his car, he had second thoughts about bringing Mr. Clyburn this money.

He was not a greedy or un-Godly man, mind you, but he suddenly realized he had entered Pastor's office and rifled through his desk to find an envelope that Pastor had never told him to look for. It wasn't that he didn't believe Mr. Clyburn was an honorable man. But he could tell by the feel of the envelope that it contained a large sum of money, and he couldn't help wondering if he would be complicit in some white-collar crime if he passed Mr. Clyburn the envelope.

The congregant got scared, talked himself out of meeting Mr. Clyburn, and early the next morning, he placed the money exactly where he found it, and then gave extra attention to cleaning Pastor's office, probably out of guilt.

Mr. Clyburn called three times within half an hour to find out what happened, so finally the congregant answered the phone and said he just couldn't do what he was asked to do. Dale was disgusted, and knew he could slip that envelope right into his inside suit jacket pocket if only he had the chance.

Problem was he had no reason to be in Pastor's office, so if he wanted to betray Pastor for money, he had better find another way. The $14,000 was back in the desk drawer, and that was the end of it.

Had this church member not gotten "cold feet" and returned the money, Chanel would not have found it, and she might not have thought there was reason to bring down her spiritual leader over a few letters from disgruntled parishioners and $800. The large sum of money, along with Harriett's confessions about covering for Pastor when bills didn't get paid, or when she smoothed things over with angry parishioners who didn't get the promised returns on their investments, caused Chanel to lose faith in Pastor Paisley.

Worse, she was so angry at his hurting his own congregants that she vowed with every fiber in her moral being to make Pastor pay for his crimes. Harriett had almost given up on balancing her boss' lies with "putting out fires" everywhere. She had already begun to look for another job when Chanel was hired. She couldn't help notice the similarity in their appearances, and thought maybe Chanel could replace her. In any case, these two women, with the same agenda against their boss, teamed up to do all they could to stop him from getting away with another dirty deed.

The women arrived at Armani's office carrying a large file of written complaints against Pastor Elvis Paisley. They also had the $800 from the petty cashbox and the $14,000 from the envelope in Pastor's desk drawer. They suspected that a criminal case might follow, and didn't want to be responsible for that kind of money.

Armani immediately recognized Chanel Bettancourt from their condo at 1400 South, and the two women exchanged pleasantries as they settled into their chairs. The assistant asked if anyone wanted coffee, but all three women declined. They wanted to get right down to business.

Armani knew Chanel as "Shay," so she called her Shay throughout the conversation. The women talked for about fifteen minutes, giving Armani a full picture of their un-Godly pastor. At first, they were referring to him in the third person using his title instead of is name.

However, once they named their boss, Armani dropped her pencil on her the legal pad on which she was taking copious notes. "Did you say Pastor Elvis Paisley? He's the man you're talking about all this time?" Just then, Armani's assistant buzzed in to announce that she needed to leave for an important meeting.

Armani almost raised her voice when she told her assistant to cancel that meeting because she was still engaged with her clients. No doubt, her assistant was puzzled because she thought she fully understood her assignment to say her boss had to leave, so that the ladies would leave.

Armani hardly heard what Shay said after that because her quick legal mind had already gone to realize the perfect solution to her dilemma about representing Katherine. She still *wouldn't* represent Katherine, but she *would* represent these women against their pastor.

Armani asked Chanel Bettancourt and Harriett Smith if they minded being deposed if she could get a court stenographer there within half an hour. They had come this far, and were determined to make their crooked boss pay for his crimes against God's children. Chanel said, *"Let the redeemed of the Lord say so. You bet we'll wait!"*

Armani assured the ladies that they had an airtight case, so their investment of time would produce the results they sought. She asked her assistant to step into the office. The assistant entered with pad and pen, looking utterly confused because she was the one receiving mixed signals from her boss. She waited for instructions.

Armani asked if there were a court stenographer in the building she shared with half a dozen lawyers. "If so, I need one as soon as possible because I need to depose both of these women." Her assistant hurried out to get the answer to Armani's question. She returned within five minutes to announce that a stenographer was just finishing up with a deposition and would be there shortly.

Armani had her assistant bring the ladies coffee and water, while she dug into the notes from the private investigator that she had practically memorized since her meeting with him yesterday. She pulled the questions to which she needed answers to be recorded into special minutes that she intended to present the same day to the judge who mentored her and cautioned her against having an affair with Dale Clyburn.

She was certain he would fit her on his calendar, and once he saw the volume of evidence against Pastor Elvis Paisley, the judge would issue the arrest warrant that law enforcement would serve on the good pastor right away.

Armani was getting ahead of herself and needed to first get this deposition completed. While she checked her notes and swallowed a cup of coffee without noticing it was probably too hot for her throat, Chanel and Harriett chatted quietly between themselves. Just as Armani looked up from her writing, the stenographer appeared, ready to go to work. Everyone moved to Armani's large conference room, and her assistant promised there would be no interruptions.

Chanel had never been deposed before, but Harriett had. Armani briefly explained the process, saying all she expected of both of them was to answer each of her questions truthfully and accurately. She then asked the questions, one by one, to which either or both women had provided answers two hours earlier.

Things moved surprisingly quickly because all the incriminating facts against Pastor Paisley were fresh in Chanel's mind. She had to refer to her files for the names of the angry parishioners who were duped by their pastor's schemes, but she never waivered, or contradicted herself when recalling the facts. She made sure to include the pastor's lustful sin of getting an underage girl pregnant and losing his wife because of that disgusting act.

Harriett had even more history against the pastor to offer, and she was able to provide information proving that her boss had engaged more than once in defrauding his congregation members. Between the statements of Chanel and Harriett, Armani had a solid case against Pastor for embezzlement, misappropriation of funds, investment fraud and having sexual relations with a minor female. She made a note that the young girl was having Pastor Paisley's illegitimate child.

She thanked the two women for their dedication and commitment, promising to keep them informed of proceedings against

Pastor Elvis Paisley and send them a transcript of their deposition. She told them to say nothing to anyone about this meeting and deposition, but to go about the normal business of running Pastor's office. She would keep everything they had brought, including all the money, to be presented as evidence in the ensuing court trial. Armani intended to call in every favor owed to her to expedite getting this trial date on the judge's docket.

Armani didn't share with Chanel and Harriett the full range of charges she intended to bring against Pastor Paisley because she knew that would involve Dale Clyburn. She had seen, when checking the balance sheets for contributions to the church, that Dale Clyburn contributed generously and often to Pastor's church.

Armani was smart enough to know that, although she was building a case against the pastor, Dale was the mastermind behind everything going on in Jamaica. Pastor Paisley had neither the savvy nor the high level connections to insert himself into drug trafficking between two countries. He was just a petty hustler.

Dale Clyburn was the big fish Armani intended to catch, but she had to be extremely careful. She intended to bring down a crooked pastor, whose confession would bring law enforcement right to the doorstep of Attorney Dale Clyburn.

Armani was beginning to feel like a large, hungry animal lying in wait for a big enough prey to eat for days. The pictures of Dale receiving a duffel full of money, and later of Pastor receiving the same kind of duffel presumably filled with expensive coffee, provided the best piece of evidence to charge both men with drug trafficking and a host of violations against Jamaican and United States laws for transporting drugs with intent to distribute for profit. Pastor's infidelity and impregnating an underage teen was the "cherry on top of the ice cream" for Armani!

Bringing down the pastor would surely cause Dale Clyburn to fall, without Armani Johnson having to compromise anything. There would be no conflict of interest now because she would be attacking "the other end of the horse!" The results would be the same, and Armani could get all the credit. Yes, she envisioned herself getting that coveted job of Lead Prosecutor for the State of Pennsylvania that Dale was drooling to receive.

What an irony that would be! Armani could get revenge as a "woman scorned," she could get justice for a wife who had been wronged, and she could do the spiritually correct thing that would save a whole congregation and maybe cause Armani Johnson to secure a place in Heaven! Was God listening to all of this?

Chapter 9
The Takedown!

Had a month passed already? The residents at 1400 South were preparing for another Happy Hour two days away. Gucci Mancini had just come into 1400 South from getting a haircut and noticed the "Happy Hour" sign posted in the elevator.

Mercedes Johannson was still angling to get Keo Staffort to fall at her feet in worship and lust. She hadn't seen or talked to Keo since the last Happy Hour, but called him to see if he wanted to join her once more. This was another chance to "get it right."

He gladly accepted the invitation, but with restrictions. The first was that he didn't like women clinging to his arm, so Mercedes was not to act as though they were a couple. Second, she wouldn't get jealous if he were talking with anyone other than her. Mercedes agreed to both exceptions to her invitation, but she had her fingers crossed behind her back because she had the mindset that no one *told* her what to do. Keo agreed to be her guest because he was hoping to meet that exotic woman he only glanced at as he was leaving the last Happy Hour. She had exceptional beauty, and if he got another chance to see her, he fully intended to engage her in conversation.

Still, if all else failed by the end of the evening, Keo was certain Mercedes would allow him to "tap her ass" later that night because he knew one thing for sure about Mercedes -- she satisfied his sexual needs without any hang ups whatsoever. She was a freak in the bedroom and he loved that about her. They understood the value of mutual pleasure. Keo decided the evening would be a "win-win," regardless of what happened that evening.

Gucci would be going to Happy Hour with Miss Dior Blue, who moved in a couple of months ago now, and attended the last Happy Hour. She was the woman Keo Staffort eyed as he was leaving that night, but Gucci gave that *"Don't even think about it!"* look to all the men drooling over Dior's exceptional beauty. He was very protective of her.

Dior was feeling better about herself, and she was more confident since Gucci showed her how to "tuck her junk" for the lingerie shoot. It went beautifully, without anyone knowing she had a penis between her legs. She had stressed herself out and almost gave up modeling when that lingerie shoot posed a threat to her identity.

But thanks to Gucci, she was more popular and more in demand than ever. Dior was away much of the past month, but it was wonderful to be back home without a modeling commitment on the evening of Happy Hour at 1400 South.

Katherine Clyburn had formally separated from Dale Clyburn because of his repeated infidelity. She had reached out to Armani Johnson to represent her in a divorce that was sure to be high profile and expensive. She was puzzled when Armani appeared to pass her off to someone else, but glad when she got the call to meet Armani the day after Happy Hour.

Katherine's friend and fellow supporter of the arts was Gucci, who invited her to join Dior and him for Happy Hour. Just the thought that Armani might have changed her mind about representing Katherine made her happy, so she was ready for Happy Hour. She might even get lucky enough to run into Armani there.

Armani had had an intense week at work, and the word "intense" was an understatement! She was poised to be the point person in a major takedown that would absolutely move her career to the next level. She was among the first to arrive at Happy Hour because she was happy all over!

Shay Bettancourt was on her way to meet Harriett Smith for dinner when she got on the elevator and saw the sign posted about Happy Hour. Shay had convinced herself that she would never attend Happy Hour because it was for the children of Satan who enjoyed the pleasures of sin.

When she got to the lobby, her friend and colleague, Harriett Smith was waiting for her. She didn't know why she mentioned to Harriett that her building was hosting its monthly Happy Hour, since she wouldn't be going. Yet the way she presented this insignificant news to Harriett caused Harriett to insist that they skip dinner and enjoy the food and drink at Happy Hour. Surely there were non-alcoholic beverages available.

Harriett liked a cocktail or two every now and then, so she managed to convince Shay that God wanted them to have some fun, after doing the right thing on behalf of the church folks whose interests they served. As Harriett gently turned Shay away from the street and in the direction of the Happy Hour Lounge, she reminded Shay that their meeting with Armani Johnson gave them reason to celebrate. Chanel Bettancourt entered the lounge for the first time since moving into 1400 South, and she seemed happy about it!

Resident Tiffany O'Brien had been out of the country since attending the last Happy Hour. She was exhausted from her trip but thought about the handsome guy she met at the last one. His name was "Keo" or "Karl" or something starting with a "K." Then she remembered how rude Mercedes had been to literally push her out of the way and drag this helpless, fine man to her table. Things would be different this time!

People were arriving at Happy Hour, and as usual, there were some familiar faces and some new faces. Gucci had been one of the first to arrive, with the lovely Miss Dior by his side. Chanel and Harriett were next. They struck up a conversation and learned that they had much in common. Harriett was in awe of

Dior, who was so much fun to be with that Harriett sat next to her while Chanel acted as though she didn't want to be there. Looking around the room actually confirmed for Chanel that she was socializing with people on that "wide path to Hell and destruction!"

Mercedes and Keo walked in and heads turned, since they made a striking couple with people whispering about how tall and sexy she was and how tall, dark and handsome he was. It was as though the red carpet was rolled out for them, since both were a bit overdressed for the occasion. Mercedes felt the need to show up the other women attending. She knew many would be coming from work wearing business attire.

Armani walked in and saw Keo with Mercedes. She went over to say hello to both of them, and Keo gave her a big hug, which Mercedes didn't like. However, Mercedes didn't intend to violate either of the two exceptions Keo placed on their date. She controlled her feelings of jealousy for the first time in her life!

Chanel was getting jealous of Harriett sitting with Dior, and Dior laughing at Harriett's korny jokes. Harriett was a real chatterbox after drinking just one cocktail. She told Dior she taught Shay's bird, Sugar, how to talk, and this pissed Chanel off. Harriett noticed Shay getting a little salty and excused herself from Dior to speak with Shay who was ready to leave because she felt out of place.

Dale Clyburn had been to Happy Hour infrequently, but he came this time as an invited guest of another resident at 1400 South. He hadn't planned to stay long, but was hoping to run into Armani, who nearly always attended. He had no idea Katherine would be there, or he would surely have come another time. Things were raw between them, as they moved towards their inevitable divorce.

Katherine hadn't seen Dale at first, but she saw Armani speaking with someone and decided to walk towards her to broach the subject of who Armani was planning to use to represent Katherine in her divorce. As Katherine walked closer, she realized that it was Dale speaking to Armani. She thought to herself that if Armani couldn't represent her, she clearly shouldn't be able to represent her husband! Or, was he there to sabotage her credibility with Armani.

In any event, Katherine planned to do something her aristocratic breeding didn't allow – raise her voice. Oh, no! Dale wasn't there to speak against Katherine, or even to speak a word about Katherine. Dale was holding Armani's arm tenderly, as if he were asking for something personal. Were *they* an item too, right under Katherine's nose?

Katherine turned around and practically ran into the ladies room after noticing Dale and Armani together. She hoped neither of them had seen her. Katherine had all sorts of thoughts running through her head, none of them good.

When she left the ladies room she noticed Armani was still there speaking with someone, but Dale was gone, so she was thankful they didn't leave together. Just as Katherine was about to approach Armani for the second time, someone else was chatting with her so Katherine thought she'd call her in the morning, even though it was Saturday.

As the evening went on, Gucci was getting bored since there wasn't anyone in the room who interested him. Katherine told Gucci and Dior she was leaving, so that made it easy for Gucci to leave too. Dior told them she had a wonderful time but she was ready to leave also. Gucci and Dior went with Katherine to the cabstand and waited for her to get a cab. Then they headed to the elevator. Happy Hour was just about over and people were leaving.

As Gucci and Dior were waiting to get on the elevator, Dior asked Gucci if he was okay and he said he was fine, but was hoping there would have been a love interest at Happy Hour. Dior asked him if he thought about on-line dating and he responded he had not. She told him he should consider it and she would set up a profile for him the next day. Well, that got him excited and he agreed to do it.

The next day, which was Saturday, Gucci was on his way up to Dior's unit when he saw Armani. He told her that Katherine Clyburn was looking for her at Happy Hour. Armani thanked him and said she would reach out to her this morning.

Gucci arrived at Dior's unit with his *Mac Book* in hand, excited about possibly of meeting someone online. They chatted a bit about how much fun they had at Happy Hour and Dior reminded Gucci of the applause he had gotten from most of the residents who came. He shared with her how touched he was by it all.

It was time to get down to business with Dior asking Gucci questions for his profile, like what he liked to do and what type person he was looking for. He told her he wanted someone who liked anything involving the fine and performing arts, and cuddling up by a cozy fireplace on a cold night.

Gucci shared with Dior that he had been in a relationship with a former cast member that lasted almost ten years. He was so in love, but then they grew apart because his partner took a job in another city and only came home once or twice a month. Finally, they separated and it broke his heart.

Gucci was close to forty years old and wanted a love that would last. Dior asked him for two photos to post with his profile, but he had so many looks, she couldn't decide which two to post. She told him to pick his favorites and he did. One was of him as a straight-looking male who resembled Tim Gunn, and the second was of him as a fierce drag queen. After all, it was an online dating site for people who enjoyed his peculiar lifestyle.

Gucci perused dozens of photos and short bios, finally asking Dior what she thought of the dude in the picture. He was hot, but was that really him? Dior and Gucci were reading his profile out loud and couldn't believe the guy lived minutes away in another high-rise building like 1400 South. Gucci was so excited about the guy that he nearly lost his mind. *"What do I do now? I mean, how do I contact him? What would I say if I met him? I'm so nervous."* Dior told him to calm down and take the first step, which was to respond online to his profile by showing interest. Gucci gleefully complied.

Armani thought hard about Gucci's comment that Katherine Clyburn was looking for her at Happy Hour. Had Katherine seen Dale Clyburn softly pressing against Armani when he touched her arm by the bar? Did Katherine know that one of Dale's conquered women was Armani Johnson?

Armani knew she would call Katherine to share the juicy information that would take down a sleezy pastor and the famous rising star, Dale Clyburn at the same time. But now she was a little uncertain about how Katherine would receive her call.

Armani was the kind of woman who took charge of situations. She was uncomfortable having ambivalent feelings about anything, so she told herself out loud that once she presented all the dirty deeds of Dale, it wouldn't matter to Katherine whether Dale did or did not have an intimate relationship with Armani. It was time to make the call.

Katherine picked up on the first ring, saying she was expecting the call. Her voice was controlled, as always, and Armani couldn't detect if Katherine had something she wanted to say first. There was a small pause in the conversation, after which Armani took control of the call.

Armani shared first everything the private investigator had presented to her about Dale Clyburn. She gave Katherine Clyburn a moment to digest it all, since Katherine had no idea Dale was involved in illegal, international drug smuggling. She expected to hear much about Dale's infidelity, and that was the information she needed to effectively proceed with divorce proceedings against her husband.

Katherine was a little unsettled when she heard Armani say that, once charges were filed, Dale would be arrested on a number of charges that would cause him to spend years in jail. She wanted him punished for the years of humiliation and embarrassment he had caused her by cheating, but she never expected or wanted to see him behind bars like a common criminal. She voiced her concern to Armani.

"Katherine, Dale's infidelity is second to the fact that he *is* a common criminal." Katherine was silent on the other end of the phone. Armani continued to lay out the way the whole case would be presented, not sure if Katherine was absorbing the magnitude of the trouble Dale was in.

"When you first called to ask me to represent you, I hesitated for two reasons. First, Dale and I have appeared in the same court, working with the same judges since he was a bankruptcy attorney. Some of the clients I prosecuted who ended up divorced needed Dale's help to get out of debt. So you see, it would be a conflict of interest for me to represent you against him."

Armani had begun to introduce Pastor Elvis Paisley's crimes into the conversation when Katherine interrupted and asked, *"What was the second reason you can't represent me? You said there were two reasons."* Armani took a sip of water that was sitting on the table next to her phone, needing time to carefully choose her words.

"Please forgive me, but I had a one-night stand with your husband some months back. It just happened, and I can honestly say it has never happened since then. I was feeling bitter about my own divorce and was on a mission to lure men from their wives and then drop them fast. It was wrong and I'm truly sorry. Now you know my second reason there would be a conflict of interest if I represented you." Katherine was speechless but Armani was relieved to have revealed that ugly secret.

Armani asked if Katherine trusted her as a professional, though she might be bruised by the personal news she just received. Katherine said she did. So Armani went on to explain that, even though she would assign a good divorce attorney to assist Katherine, she would be involved in all the proceedings because she intended to prosecute the corrupt Pastor Elvis Paisley, who was directly connected to Dale Clyburn.

Armani filled Katherine in on all the details, ending by saying that her first priority was to bring down the no good pastor, but Dale Clyburn would fall harder because he had more to lose. Armani kept to herself the small fact that, should Dale end up in jail and Armani rise to a famous height as a lawyer, she should be in line for the prestigious position that would never go to him. Armani didn't wait for Katherine to thank her for any of this news before she intended to end the call by saying she would be in touch soon to introduce Katherine's new lawyer to her.

Katherine showed the slightest bit of urgency when she said, *"Don't hang up yet, Armani because I've got something I want to say. Truthfully, by the time you had your one-night-stand with my husband, our marriage was pretty much over. I thank you for having enough guilt or shame to be with him just once.*

Nevertheless, I never understood why some women covet other women's husbands. In case you're wondering if I saw Dale squeeze your arm at Happy Hour, I did. I chose not to confront either of you because I was getting a divorce. Still, I ran into the bathroom because it bothered me. I'm over all that today, and I'm ready to move forward with your takedown of that evil pastor and my husband."

Pastor Paisley was in Jamaica on his second trip. He felt much more at ease this time. As he lay on his bed watching a little television, the doorbell rang. He hadn't ordered room service, but eagerly opened the door to find a young, beautiful and sexy girl carrying a tray of champagne and strawberries. She said with a slight accent, *"All of this is for you."* Pastor immediately got a hard on, and made no attempt to hide it when he invited the girl inside. Before closing the door, he looked left and right in the hallway, just in case someone was watching. The coast was clear!

By the time he closed the door, the girl had poured two glasses of champagne, and was pushing a strawberry into his mouth. He let the juice drip down his chin, and she immediately licked it off.

Within half a minute, both were in his bed beginning to undress. She unhooked her bra, rather than wait for him to clumsily try to get it off. Her soft, pink blouse was already on the floor. Pastor could not believe how perky her breasts were, but of course they would not have been affected by gravity at the age of fifteen or sixteen! He licked and bit them as much as he wanted, while she pulled at his ears and hair.

They were in for an amazing time when the Jamaica Constabluary Force (JCF) and the U. S. Drug Enforcement Administration (DEA) undercover officers came bursting into his hotel room yelling, *"Hands up!"* He couldn't believe what was happening because he literally had his hands up this young girl's pink skirt and was about to take off her matching pink panties. The girl attempted to cover her breasts and screamed uncontrollably, as one of the officers threw a towel at her so she could cover up.

Pastor Paisley's pants were unbuttoned and unzipped when the order was given, so when he put his hands above his head, his pants fell around his ankles. His underwear was definitely secular! He and the girl got down on the floor while guns were pointed at their heads. Pastor couldn't believe this was happening, as he cursed under his breath. The girl was clearly underage, and kept screaming for him to do something.

His head felt like it was exploding and his face felt hot. He remembered resisting the affection of a woman who approached him at the hotel Happy Hour on his first trip to Jamaica. He knew he was supposed to keep a low profile.

Suddenly, he wondered if the girl who literally showed up at his door carrying champagne and strawberries was a setup. He wondered why a beautiful young girl wanted to bring him food and drink, and then throw herself on his bed and begin to undress herself. What else could the good Pastor do except help her finish undressing?

A sickening feeling came over him as he fully grasped the severity of his predicament. Not only was he getting ready to take advantage of a minor in another country, but also he had two duffel bags full of the finest Jamaican coffee that he expected to carry on the plane to the USA.

Pastor thought for a second about the attorney Dale told him to call in case he got into trouble, and now he was in big trouble. He carried the number in his pants pocket, but he would need to pull up his pants in order to retrieve the number from his pocket. He asked politely if he could pull his pants up, and a young officer nodded affirmatively.

The JCF told him he was under arrest and there were dozens of search warrants being issued across the island relative to drug trafficking with intent to sell and consume, and transporting drugs outside of Jamaica. Seems they had been following Dale Clyburn for two months, and this was the day they had enough evidence to arrest him.

However, two trips ago, Pastor Paisley replaced Dale Clyburn in making the drug runs, so he was the unlucky one caught in the sting operation. They searched his room and found the duffel bags with *"Blue Mountain Jamaican Coffee"* inside. They told him once they got to the precinct he could make one call, just like in America. But right now, he needed to put his hands behind his back so they could handcuff him for security purposes.

As the large number of police escorted Pastor Elvis Paisley to the police car to bring him to the station, a dozen television cameras were flashing, with reporters shoving microphones in Pastor's face and asking more questions than he could comprehend, much less answer responsibly. The young girl was seen on camera running away half dressed and barefoot, her long, thick hair covering her bare breasts.

Pastor couldn't hide his face, so he dropped his head as close to his chest as possible. That caused him to notice a wet circle in his groin area. He didn't even realize that he had urinated on himself when he heard, *"Hands up!"* He wanted to cry, but held himself together because all those television cameras were showing his face all over Jamaica, and probably in America as well. His career as the leader of the flock was over. His livelihood was over. His fraudulent "get rich" schemes were over. Hell, his life was over, but he was too cowardly to end it!

As soon as Pastor got to the police station and was released temporarily from his handcuffs, he frantically reached into his pocket to find the phone number of the person who would end his nightmare withn the hour. He made the call, watching his hands trembling the whole time he was dialing. A recording said the number was not in service. Now Pastor cried and didn't care who saw his tears flowing.

He demanded to make a second call, but was denied. Two local reporters had entered the police precinct and were rolling their film when Pastor Elvis Paisley had a breakdown on camera. *"I need to call Dale Clyburn. He's the one you want, not me. He tried to steal $14,000 from me. Wait! I mean he didn't do that, but he promised I would be protected from prosecution if I got caught doing what he did lots more times than I did. You want Dale Clyburn, not a smalltime pastor who never did anything against the law before."*

Armani Johnson was first to learn of the arrest because her private investigator called to say the pastor they were about to serve with arrest papers was already arrested in Jamaica. He told her to turn on her television to CNN and she could witness the pathetic jackleg preacher crying in front of millions of people.

Armani immediately turned on her TV to see what those two reporters were recording live from Jamaica. She heard Dale's name five times within as many minutes. Pastor went from standing up and shouting to kneeling and screaming like a wounded animal caught in a sophisticated trap. It was a pitiful sight to behold.

Armani quickly called Katherine, and then Chanel and Harriett so all could watch the sobbing rant of Pastor Paisley on international television. No doubt some of his parishioners and maybe even his estranged wife were watching too.

While Armani, Chanel and Harriett were probably glad Pastor Paisley was getting his just due, Katherine was likely thinking ahead to Dale's arrest. She knew her husband would never fall to the floor and grovel, nor would he cry like an infant. She thought she hated him, but the thought of him in this much trouble kindled feelings of love inside her again. Getting a divorce was insignificant, next to drug trafficking. She couldn't bring herself to call Dale, but knew someone would.

Dale was in his office working a case when he got a call from his Jamaican contact telling him the "Preacher Man" was just arrested for a bunch of crimes, and he was on television squealing like a pig about Dale Clyburn. Oh, yeah, he gave Dale's first and last name, hoping Dale's arrest would free Pastor. That was never going to happen.

Dale couldn't resist turning on his television, and he caught the last words of Pastor Paisley before he was led away to jail. *"Dale Clyburn is the Devil who made me do it!"* Dale sunk back into his tufted leather chair, wondering what that little weasel did to get caught. He knew it was a matter of time before the authorities would be coming for him, so he stopped working and locked his office door.

Dale wasn't going to jail, nor was he going to be humiliated on television like Pastor. He had put many criminals behind bars, and therefore, he feared that he could – no, he *would* be raped or killed in jail. His career was over, just when he reached his peak of success. He had made a mess of his marriage and had to suffer the consequences of that. If he allowed himself to be arrested, he would surely go to jail. There was only one option that was sure to keep him out of jail – suicide!

He didn't know that the drug enforcement agencies from both countries had teamed up to bring him down, but he had to admit that the old saying, *"crime doesn't pay"* is true. He stepped in front of his bathroom mirror and looked himself squarely in the eyes without blinking. *"Well, you Devil, you can just come and get me because I'm not afraid of you. I almost welcome you here!"*

He kept staring at himself in the mirror, regretting everything about his life, and wishing he had someone to listen to those regrets. Dale decided to end this nightmare with the dignity of a "man's man" like the actor James Cagney did in his prison movies. He went to his desk drawer where he kept a *Smith & Wesson* revolver. He returned to his desk with the gun in his hand, and carefully placed it in the middle of his desk. Nervously, he circled the desk a few times, wondering if he had the nerve to take his life. Then, he sat down, aimed the gun at his head and pulled the trigger.

The clerk who worked for Dale heard a loud bang and tried to open the door but it was locked. He called "911" and they responded quickly. They had to break down the office door with axes and hammers, and when it fell, they rushed inside to see Dale's head buried in a pile of legal papers on his desk, with blood covering the whole desk and his lifeless body slumped over his desk.

The EMT's tried everything to revive him because he had a weak pulse. They rushed him to the hospital, leaving the office clerk in shock. Before the clerk could compose himself, the DEA officers appeared, weapons drawn, and kicked in the door to Dale's office, which was now an active crime scene. When they saw all the blood, they backed up slowly, closed the door, and left to report that he wasn't there, but was likely hurt badly.

Between the ambulance and the DEA, it was impossible to keep reporters from joining the crowd in Dale's outer office. But there was yellow tape across the doorway to Dale's office because it was now a crime scene. Reporters took advantage of the open doorway and snapped numerous pictures of Dale's bloody desk, chair and floor. The photos were gruesome, which meant every local and national media outlet scooped them up to increase their newspaper sales or television ratings. The office clerk was too traumatized to utter a word when those reporters shoved cameras and microphones in his face. So they speculated wildly about what must have occurred. They were correct about the fact that Dale Clyburn had been shot and was in severely critical condition.

Armani and Chanel and Harriett had not turned off their televisions, when they heard: *"Breaking News: Prominent Attorney Dale Clyburn has been shot and is in severely critical condition. He's not expected to live. No further details about the circumstances surrounding this horrible tragedy are known at this time."*

No one expected this turn of events. Armani was too shaken at that moment to resume preparing her case against Pastor Paisley, which was supposed to insure that Dale Clyburn went to jail along with Pastor. She felt flushed and went to the bathroom to wash her face. Instead, she threw up.

Armani was startled to hear her phone ringing. It was Katherine, hysterical over the news that Dale was shot. She asked Armani if she thought it was a self-inflicted wound or if someone who wanted to silence him shot him.

Armani felt like all the energy had been sucked out of her. She weakly responded that she didn't know the answer.

Katherine asked if it would compromise her case if she went to the hospital to get the full story. Armani sensed that Katherine needed to be by her husband's side and that maybe there would be no divorce proceedings – that is, if he lived. The media experts predicted he would die within the hour.

Chapter 10
Happy Ending!

Gucci Mancini, with the able assistance of Miss Dior Blue, had set up an online profile, where he said he was seeking love and a longstanding relationship. He got a response back from someone who lived close by named Serge Aura, and they set a date and time to meet. Gucci couldn't believe what a gorgeous hunk Serge was, and he hoped Serge looked that good in person. He was so excited about his new love prospect, thinking maybe this could be "the one!"

Miss Dior Blue had been traveling the world modeling, and she was on numerous magazine covers. Her agent told her she had a request about Dior possibly being a *Sports Illustrated* model. That excited her because one of Dior's desires was to be on that magazine cover.

Dior began a relationship with the head of the maintenance company servicing 1400

South and half a dozen office buildings around town. She had been saving her money so she could have reconstructive surgery, and once she had the surgery she would reveal to the world that she was transgender. She felt she should be the voice for those who were ridiculed by society, just like her.

Mercedes Johannson thought she was in love with Keo Staffort, but she knew it was strictly a sexual relationship on his part. She decided to cut all ties with him, since at the last Happy Hour he couldn't stop looking at Dior Blue, the high and mighty fashion model. True, Mercedes had agreed not to be jealous if he looked at other women, but she wanted him to look at only her so he could love only her. Instead, he disrespected her, so it was time to move on and find someone who could handle her kind of beauty and independence.

Mercedes was promoted from "flight attendant" to "Cabin Manager" or "Purser," which meant she oversaw a number of flight attendants. In her new role, she had more time to flirt with unsuspecting male passengers while maintaining the professional attitude that got her the promotion.

Keo Staffort had fallen for Miss Dior Blue and was ready to marry her after meeting her at Happy Hour. There was something about her that intrigued him and he couldn't figure out why she wasn't interested in him. He had set his eyes on so many women, and thought he loved Armani for a while. But he never felt his insides churning until he beheld Miss Dior Blue.

He would do anything to win that prize because, unlike Mercedes, Dior could keep his eyes from ever wandering again. Dior had her own plans and secrets, and didn't care to share them with Keo Staffort.

Chanel Bettancourt and Harriett Smith became more than friends and their lives changed after the takedown of Pastor Paisley, with help from Attorney Armani Johnson. Harriett's lease was up, so she moved in with Chanel, who had two bedrooms. Harriett taught the parrot, Sugar, to ask Chanel, *"Where ya been?" "When ya comin' back?"* Chanel was not amused!

Armani regained her focus on having Pastor Elvis Paisley extradited to the United States to stand trial for his crimes here, after which he would return to Jamaica to face additional charges and a stiff prison sentence. Jamaican prisons were harsher than ours, so he'd have "a lifetime" to confess his sins before God and try to redeem his soul.

Pastor Paisley's parishioners learned of the scandal and were devastated by the news. They were sad for the pastor, whom they believed brought them the Word of God until he became greedy for money. Some were even willing to forgive him for the indiscretion with the teen congregant, but none could forgive his collective sins.

They were in search of a real man of God to provide them spiritual nourishment. But until a replacement pastor was found, the church was closed. Chanel Bettancourt walked by the boarded up church building on her way to her new job as Executive Assistant to Armani Johnson, Esquire.

Armani was able to get the judge who cared most for her to add the Paisley trial to his calendar, and he signed the arrest warrant that would cause Pastor Paisley to return to the United States immediately. The press was everywhere Armani was, because they knew she was the "go to" person for up-to-the-minute news about Paisley. They also hounded her about her future, now that she was the clear frontrunner to rise high in the legal and political world.

The press kept watch outside Katherine Clyburn's home, and a few reporters bothered hospital personnel for word of Dale's condition. Katherine Clyburn was frightened, devastated, confused and miserable. She was hoping against hope that her husband would live, and yet sorry she never got her divorce.

She hated what he had done to her, but was overwhelmed at the life he lived outside of their marriage. Once she learned from the head physician at the hospital that Dale suffered a self-inflicted gunshot wound to the head, Katherine prayed God would not send him straight to hell. Suicide was a sin in nearly all religions, but she was a devout Catholic, where the penalties were clear.

While all this was going on, a notice was posted in the elevator and the mailroom at 1400 South that there would be one last Happy Hour the following Friday because the lounge was being closed for renovation. The buzz among the residents was all about Dale Clyburn and Pastor Elvis Paisley. No one could believe how much money was involved in drug smuggling, but they agreed that using coffee as the cover was a clever idea.

Armani did, in fact, get the appointment to the top job as Lead Prosecutor for the State of Pennsylvania. Her really expensive services were in high demand. But she was drained after the trial of Pastor Paisley. She wished she could have gotten the honest parishioners at Paisley's church a financial settlement, but nonetheless, justice was served.

Chanel and Harriett attended the last Happy Hour as a couple. Harriett continued to teach Sugar, the parrot, a few more words to add to her increasing sensual vocabulary. Harriett wanted to get another parrot as company for Sugar, but Shay told her Sugar was quite enough!

Dale Clyburn was on life support, and there would be no headlines unless he either died or emerged from his coma. Katherine Clyburn sat faithfully by his side for a week, but then realized she had to move on with her life until something final happened with her husband.

Armani invited Katherine Clyburn to the last Happy Hour, wanting both of them to go somewhere quiet and warm for some much-needed rest and a little fun. She thought of Jamaica. Hell no! It would be Aruba! Katherine gladly accepted, being completely drained emotionally. The two would discover a lasting friendship by the end of the trip.

Neither Mercedes nor Keo were able to attend this Happy Hour, but Gucci came with Miss Dior. After realizing that his online hunk of a man lived close to 1400 South, Gucci decided their first meeting would be at this Happy Hour. The handsome and confident Serge Aura accepted the invitation and both men were happy by the end of Happy Hour. As everyone was leaving, Serge paused to read the neon sign over the bar: *"Hate your job or your life? There's a support group for that called HAPPY HOUR!"*

At the beginning of the trial of the poor, pitiful Pastor Paisley, he got the shocking news that Dale Clyburn had shot himself and was on life support. All he wanted when he was first arrested was to see Dale "hang" in Pastor's place, but now the full weight of his own sins fell upon his shoulders. He deserved every bit of his punishment in two countries.

Pastor Paisley dropped to his knees in his prison cell, burying his face in his pillow to muffle his sobs of repentance. *"Father, God, you once chose me to bring healing and salvation to a flock in need of a leader. I answered the call without hesitation, saying,*

'Here am I, Lord.' My heart was filled with Holy Spirit and all I wanted was to do your will."

He reached for the *Holy Bible* on his bed and opened it to the Book of Judges 16: *"Then Samson called to the LORD, saying, 'O Lord GOD, remember me, I pray! Strengthen me, I pray, just this once, O God....' So the dead that he killed at his death were more than he had killed in his life."* Pastor Elvis Paisley was genuinely remorseful. *"If You will allow me to serve You again through a prison ministry, I vow that my latter life will be greater than all my previous years. Amen. Amen.*

THE END

ABOUT THE AUTHOR

Valerie Small was born in Philadelphia, PA. She graduated from Bok Technical High School, after which she attended Temple University with a major in Journalism.

Val is married, has two sons and two granddaughters, and is a temporary foster mother of a pre-school child. She resides in Orlando, FL since 1997. Val volunteers with the Salvation Army and is part of the Disaster Relief Team.

Val has worked thirty years for NBA Legend, Julius "Dr. J" Erving, running the day-to-day operations for the The Erving Group, which was created in 1979. Val joined the group in 1985, mentored by V.P./Business Manager Ray Wilson.

When Dr. Erving became Senior Vice President for Orlando Magic, Val was his Personal and Executive Assistant. She organized the Julius Erving "Sweet 16" Party when he retired from the Philadelphia 76ers, and The Clash of the Legends featuring Julius Erving and Kareem Abdul-Jabbar, with proceeds going to the Cory Marvin Erving Foundation (CMEF).

Valerie Small is available for book readings and signings, and motivational and keynote speaking engagements. She can be reached at ladyveewrites@gmail.com.